"You shouldn't be doing this..."

Kennedy grinned in response and flicked the button on her shorts open. The sound of her zipper, metal grinding against metal, was loud in Asher's ears.

"Nope. You can't touch."

"What?" he asked in disbelief. The woman was giving him a striptease and expected him to keep his hands to himself?

She was crazy. Or wickedly, wickedly devious.

Or both.

"You get through the rest of these interview questions without hesitating and then you can have your reward."

How was he supposed to resist with her standing in front of him in nothing but red lace panties and a matching bra?

He was human. He'd been fighting his desire for too long. He couldn't fight anymore.

"Then you better hurry with those questions before I say to hell with it and give you exactly what you're asking for..."

Dear Reader,

It's a little bittersweet to see the end of my SEALs of Fortune series. Over the past year, I've enjoyed working with these amazing men and the headstrong women who fall for them, immersing myself in their intense, honorable and sometimes hectic world.

At the core of this series is a family that's formed not necessarily by blood, but brotherhood, battle and shared values. That is no more evident than in Asher Reynolds's story. A man used to being left behind, Asher learns that he's worth choosing, worth wanting and worth respecting. Kennedy Duchane is just the strong-willed woman to teach him that valuable lesson. Beneath their verbal clashes is an attraction neither of them wants to admit. A vulnerability that puts them on edge and forces them to acknowledge that people and situations can't always be controlled. The question is, can they both let go of their pasts long enough to appreciate what's right in front of them?

I hope you enjoy *Under Pressure*! If you've missed any of the other SEALs of Fortune books, check them out to get a glimpse into Kennedy and Asher's history, and learn more about the family they've formed with Jackson Duchane, Loralei Lancaster, Knox McLemore and Avery Walsh.

I'd love to hear from you at kirasinclair.com, or come chat with me on Twitter, @KiraSinclair.

Best wishes,

Kira

Kira Sinclair

Under Pressure

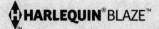
HARLEQUIN® BLAZE™

ISBN-13: 978-0-373-79872-8

Under Pressure

Copyright © 2015 by Kira Bazzel

Printed in U.S.A.

www.Harlequin.com

Kira Sinclair writes emotional, passionate contemporary romances. A double winner of the National Readers' Choice Award, her first foray into writing fiction was for a high school English assignment. Nothing could dampen her enthusiasm...not even being forced to read the love story aloud to the class. Writing about sexy heroes and strong women has always excited her. She lives with her two beautiful daughters in north Alabama. Kira loves to hear from readers at kirasinclair.com.

Books by Kira Sinclair

HARLEQUIN BLAZE

Bring It On

Take It Down

Rub It In

The Risk-Taker

She's No Angel

The Devil She Knows

Captivate Me

Testing the Limits

Bring Me to Life

SEALs of Fortune

Under the Surface

In Too Deep

To get the inside scoop on Harlequin Blaze and its talented writers, be sure to check out BlazeAuthors.com.

All backlist available in ebook format.

Visit the Author Profile page at Harlequin.com for more titles.

My life has been a little crazy over the past year, a roller coaster of experiences and emotions. But there are a handful of people I know I can count on to be there for me when I'm at my weakest. This book is dedicated to Andrea Laurence, Kimberly Lang, Dani Wade and Marilyn Baxter. I often feel like I'm spread thin and you guys get the shaft, but when I hit a wall and feel like I can't keep going, just knowing you're close pushes me to do it anyway. Love you!

1

"YOU'RE MY ONLY OPTION." Sure, the words might have sounded like a plea for help, but that wasn't how Kennedy Duchane meant them. At all.

She glared at the man in front of her, ready to use whatever means necessary to compel his cooperation. Despite being a foot shorter and roughly a hundred pounds lighter, she wasn't opposed to dropping Asher Reynolds to his knees if that became necessary.

She had an older brother who also happened to be a former navy SEAL—he'd taught her plenty over the years.

Asher's mouth formed a lazy smile. "Aww, cupcake, we both know that isn't true. I'm sure the devil would be happy to fix whatever's got your panties in a twist if you just ask nicely."

Kennedy blinked. As far as she was concerned, Asher Reynolds *was* the devil, but she had no intention of asking him for anything, nicely or otherwise. She was demanding. He might be her boss—or one of them—but not even that was going to save him from doing what she needed this time.

Florida sunshine poured through the window at Asher's back, gilding him in a way that was frustrating and enticing all at once. She could practically feel it warming her skin and wished she were on one of their beautiful Jacksonville beaches right now instead of in this office arguing—again—with the frustrating man.

But wishing wasn't going to take care of the problem. Taking a deep breath, Kennedy marched the rest of the way into his office. As always, he was sprawled out, wireless keyboard in his lap, feet propped up on the corner of his desk. She had no idea how he accomplished anything. But he did.

Kennedy had to give him that, even if it did burn a little. He was brilliant at business. And, given a different set of circumstances, she would have loved to learn from him.

Knocking his black motorcycle boots off the desk, Kennedy relished the way Asher's body rocked back in the chair as his feet connected with the floor.

"Seriously, you know you're going to have to do this, right?"

He frowned up at her out of those moss-green eyes that had the ability to make her feel like a butterfly pinned to a board.

Plopping her butt on to the desk corner she'd just cleared, Kennedy crossed her arms over her chest and settled in. This was one fight she would not lose.

"We leave for the Bahamas tomorrow whether you like it or not."

"Since when do you issue orders, baby girl? I'm pretty sure I'm still the one signing your paycheck."

"Wrong, Jackson signs the paychecks, but even if you did, you're still going. I need you on this documentary."

The words grated a little coming out of her throat, but they were true. She did need him. Desperately.

Several months ago, her brother, Jackson, had discovered a sunken Civil War ship lost for more than one hundred and fifty years. The company Jackson, Asher and Knox owned together, Trident Diving and Salvage, now had exclusive recovery rights. If the rumors of gold in the ship were true, it would put an end to their financial worries for good. In the meantime, she hoped the documentary about Trident's discovery and salvaging of the *Chimera* would keep them in the media spotlight and bring in new clients.

"I don't think so," Asher drawled, his Southern accent smooth as aged whiskey. "Get one of the other guys to do it. Someone who's actually spent time on the salvage team. Ryan, Juan, Drake."

She was already shaking her head before he'd even gotten one name past his lips. "No, no and no. I promised the production company Jackson. I've already had to do some fancy footwork in order for them to accept you. Luckily, your face is rather appealing and makes up for your smart mouth."

"Aw, shucks. You're gonna make me blush."

"Shut it," Kennedy growled, knocking the pointed toe of her shoe against his shin. The tap wasn't hard enough to even leave a mark, let alone a bruise. But she couldn't quite suppress the small, petty spurt of satisfaction when he winced.

"I'm telling dad." Asher mock whined.

"Go right ahead. I'm pretty sure he loves me more."

Asher let out a huff, the first sign that he was really taking her seriously. "Jackson can leave Loralei in charge for a couple weeks."

"You know we can't spare either of them right now."

It was bad timing. There was no doubt. But Kennedy couldn't muster the energy to regret Jackson and Lora-lei's newest discovery, several clustered artifacts found at the bottom of the Mediterranean. They were all sali-vating over the possibility that this new find could in-dicate a lost ancient city. Since they'd been challenged for their rights to the *Chimera*, they were taking no chances with their latest score. They had to keep it quiet until the paperwork was in place. And Jackson needed to stay at the site to protect their claim.

"What about Knox?"

Kennedy sighed, allowing herself one brief moment of disappointment before she pushed it away. Working with Knox would have been a breeze. And come with the added bonus of Avery Walsh, a nautical archeolo-gist with years of experience.

Goddamn the flu.

"It's you, Asher. Don't make me call Jackson and Knox."

As far as she could tell, they were the only people in the world who could compel Asher to do anything. Now that she thought about it, in the two years she'd known him, Kennedy had never heard him speak of any other friends or family. Trident appeared to be his entire life. The man didn't even have a pet.

Asher leaned forward, sliding the keyboard he'd been holding onto the top of his desk. "Trust me when I say you need to find someone else."

She'd known, the moment she'd realized Asher was the only option she had, that he wouldn't want to do it. She'd anticipated his refusal, his arguments and hadn't counted out the possibility of a full-blown tantrum.

What she hadn't expected was the earnest, intense way he stared at her as he evenly announced he wasn't the man for the job. For a second she almost believed he had a valid reason for refusing.

But then she realized who she was talking to and swallowed back the unwelcome well of concern. Asher didn't deserve it. He was playing her, nothing more.

Leaning forward, Kennedy chucked him under the chin. "Sorry, frogman, time to take one for the team." And then turned to leave.

Stopping at the door, she tossed a warning glance over her shoulder. "Our plane leaves at nine in the morning. If I have to hunt you down, I'll make you regret it."

ASHER UNCLENCHED HIS fists from the arms of his chair. Blood rushed back into his fingers.

He could feel the tension building inside his body. Just the thought of what she was asking him to do…

First, his shoulders and back tightened. Then his stomach cramped, tying into knots any sailor would be proud of. His throat closed up. His mouth went dry. And his tongue suddenly felt useless, four times bigger than his mouth.

Familiar symptoms for a major problem he couldn't seem to conquer no matter how hard he tried. His body reacted the same way to any stressful situation. Had since he was six years old.

The sensations were so familiar. Straight out of his childhood nightmares. The memories, the taunts. The humiliation and embarrassment. Everyone staring as his mouth stumbled and refused to form the words his brain was screaming.

He was a goddamned navy SEAL. Was the toughest of the tough, could stare down terrorists, defuse bombs and take a bullet with barely a flinch. But this, this one weakness he'd been struggling with for so long, he couldn't master.

Over the years he'd perfected avoidance tactics, successfully extricating himself from situations likely to trigger his speech impediment. Hell, even his best friends weren't aware of his issue.

And he wanted to keep it that way.

Unfortunately, Kennedy's request—no, demand—was going to blow that possibility straight out of the water.

And to put the icing on this craptastic cake, she would be there to witness his humiliation.

There was no doubt in Asher's mind that just her presence was going to make the situation ten times worse. There was something about Kennedy Duchane that got under his skin.

Her scent. Her take-charge attitude. Her ability to call him on his bullshit and the way she stared at him out of those whiskey-brown eyes.

The fact that there was no way on God's green earth he could touch her even though that was the only thing he wanted whenever she was close.

Even now, the scent of Kennedy's perfume lingered in his office, taunting him long after she was gone.

It bothered him, the way she could affect him without even trying. The way his body always seemed to overrule his brain.

Kennedy was off-limits. His best friend's little sister, his employee, not to mention nine years younger than he was. There were so many reasons to keep his hands to himself, but the more time he spent with her the harder that seemed to be.

His solution was to avoid Kennedy as much as he could. A little difficult considering she worked for the company he co-owned. So when that wasn't possible, he did his best to push her away with snarky comments.

Lucky for him, she was easy to manipulate. Because he suspected if she ever realized how much power she held over him…she wouldn't hesitate to use it.

And he could admit he'd probably earned her wrath.

The project she was ready to throw him headfirst into was a bad idea on multiple fronts. How the hell had he ended up in this situation?

More importantly, how could he extricate himself before everyone in his life discovered the secret he'd been hiding for years?

Picking up the phone, Asher dialed Knox's cell.

He didn't bother with pleasantries, just launched straight into the attack when his friend answered. "What the hell, man? You on death's door?"

"Feels that way," Knox croaked.

"Bullshit. I've seen you crawl through mud with a bullet hole oozing blood. I had a temp of one-oh-one when we took that little village outside of Kandahar. Suck it up, buttercup. We need you."

"I'm not—" Knox's words cut off abruptly, and he could hear the sound of scuffling in the background before a smooth, soft voice came on the line. "Asher, whatever you want, the answer is no."

"Firecracker," Asher said, a grin tugging at his lips.

Now, Avery Walsh was a woman he liked. And it wasn't just because she delighted in giving his friend shit. That had a lot to do with his affection for her, but she was a force to be reckoned with all on her own. "How've you been?"

"I'm wonderful, but Knox feels like crap."

"So he was saying."

"I've already talked with Kennedy." He could hear the suppressed humor in Avery's voice and wanted to hate her for it, but couldn't quite muster up the energy.

Damn Kennedy for her organizing tendencies and preemptive strike.

"Listen," he started, modulating his voice into a smooth tone with only a hint of cajoling thrown into the mix.

"Don't even start," Avery warned. Asher wasn't sure he liked the fact that the women in the group talked to each other on a regular basis. It was definitely becoming a problem for him.

"You're not getting out of this one, Ash. Not this time." She didn't even bother to hide the laughter warming her words. He probably should have taken offense, but didn't.

"I'm glad you think this is funny," he drawled, leaning back and propping his feet up into their normal position on the edge of his desk.

His entire body relaxed, sinking down into the forgiving leather of his office chair.

This was familiar territory, bantering with a beautiful woman. Safe and comfortable, especially because he knew nothing he did or said could tempt Avery away from the man she loved.

"Trust me, it's funny as hell," she said. "Your pretty face is finally working against you."

"What's that supposed to mean?"

"Come on, you know you're beautiful, Asher. And you use it to your advantage."

Shit, he didn't see anything wrong with that. The navy had taught them all to use the assets they'd been given. He was just following orders, nothing more, nothing less.

"It's gratifying to see it turned against you for a change," Avery continued.

"You know, I really liked you, doc…before you turned into such a ball buster."

Avery chuckled, completely unfazed. "Your charm isn't going to get you out of this one, sailor. Sorry."

It had been a long shot, but one he'd had to at least try. Because the alternative… A cold wash of dread rushed through his body.

Saying goodbye to Avery, Asher disconnected and stared at his computer screen without actually seeing what was there.

Shit. He was out of options.

He'd stared down heartless terrorists. Watched as boys who were barely strong enough to hold the guns they were using died in a war they likely didn't understand. He'd jumped out of perfectly functioning airplanes and plunged his body into raging cold seas. Putting his own life on the line was nothing new. Danger and fear were nothing new. That kind of stress he could easily deal with, because he was equipped to handle it. Felt comfortable and confident in his skills and training.

So why the hell couldn't he conquer this?

The only easy day was yesterday.

Today, the Navy SEAL motto was cold comfort. Taking a deep breath, Asher forced himself to relax his body. He would find a way to make this work.

Kennedy hadn't given him any other choice.

And he'd be damned if he'd let her see him at his weakest.

KENNEDY HALF EXPECTED to have to track Asher down, which was why she'd told him nine when their plane really didn't leave until ten. Padding in extra time for disaster had simply been good strategy.

Until the man actually strolled up to the gate at eight.

She should have been relieved. She wasn't. Because that meant they had an hour and a half to kill sitting outside their gate before their flight boarded.

Asher folded himself into the uncomfortable chair next to her, the bench kind with chrome arms sticking out to delineate each seat from the next. Why hadn't he taken one chair down?

His shoulders rubbed against hers, forcing Kennedy to shift into the opposite corner to get away from him.

The flight was going to be hell.

"Nine, huh," he murmured in that deep, dark voice that always managed to send a shiver down her spine.

The only outward reaction Kennedy allowed was for her mouth to tighten into a frown.

"I suppose I deserved that," he said, stretching his legs out until they practically touched the bench on the opposite side of the aisle.

He was tall, at least a couple of inches over six feet. With wide shoulders and a narrow waist that tapered into the most perfect tight ass she'd ever seen. He could wear the hell out of a pair of jeans. Or a business suit. Or a wet suit.

Wait, what had they been talking about?

"Yes, you did. I'm just glad I didn't have to chase after you."

The minute the words left her mouth, Kennedy regretted them. She held her breath, waiting for the smart-ass comment she knew was coming.

"Darlin', if I'd known you wanted a chase, I'd have been happy to oblige."

Kennedy raked him with the sharp edge of her gaze. "I don't chase."

Asher's lips tugged up at the edges. "No, I can't imagine you would, baby girl."

God, she hated when he called her that. But she'd given up reprimanding him for the slight a long time ago.

She needed to pull this conversation—and the entire trip—back to center. And the fastest method for that was reminding him—and herself—just what their purpose was.

Reaching into her bag, Kennedy pulled out the glossy dossier she'd prepared for Asher and handed it to him.

He took it, his big fingers tangling with hers for a moment before finally letting go. Asher stared at her for several seconds and then glanced down, flipping through the papers.

She'd taken the time to write up a detailed agenda for the trip and included that along with a draft script. She'd thrown in some background information on the production team and even included a copy of the proposal she'd submitted when pitching them the idea for the show.

He studied it, silent and still. And yet, Kennedy could

practically feel the energy vibrating beneath his skin. Or was that just her imagination?

Closing the cover, Asher let out a low whistle. "You need a hobby."

"No, I don't."

His eyes cut to her above the frosted edge of the plastic she'd placed on the front and back of the document. He held her gaze, to the point where she wanted to squirm beneath the pressure of his scrutiny. But she wouldn't.

That was the thing about Asher that she'd learned early on…he was excellent at spotting and exploiting weaknesses while keeping any he might possess firmly under wraps. She worked damn hard at making sure not to reveal any to him. Or any more.

It was bad enough that he'd been an unwanted part of the most humiliating night of her life.

No matter how hard she worked or how competent she was, she didn't think she'd ever live down that night. At least not with Asher.

"Look, this shouldn't be difficult for you. You're charming and gorgeous."

"Thanks."

Kennedy ignored the self-confident grin that curled his lips. "The camera will love you. You've got the script. Do me a favor and look over it on the plane."

Maybe that would keep him occupied for a while and out of her personal space.

His gaze raked across her body, lingering on the low V-cut neckline of the T-shirt she'd thrown on this morning. It was unremarkable and not her normal office attire. But they were heading for Nassau where they'd meet up with the *Amphitrite* before sailing out to open sea.

She would not apologize for dressing comfortably, even if the way he was watching her made her regret not putting on the business clothes she typically used as armor.

His chest rose and fell as he leaned farther into her. Kennedy wanted to move away, but her body wouldn't listen to the commands her brain was screaming.

God, he smelled good. That was the only clear thought running through her overwhelmed brain.

"Are you sure that's what you want to do on the plane, Kennedy? I'm sure we can think of…more pleasant ways to pass the time."

She blinked. Her body swayed. Somehow her hand ended up planted in the center of his chest. His wide, strong, hard chest.

A jangling sound startled her, breaking the spell. She jerked back, realizing it was the ringtone on her phone.

A smirk tugged at the edges of Asher's lips even as a single, wicked eyebrow crooked up. The man knew exactly what kind of effect he had on women. Any woman with a pulse.

Irritation flaming through her, Kennedy snatched up her phone and said, "Hello," without even looking at her screen.

"Ms. Duchane? This is Simone from Masters, Dillon and Cooper."

Kennedy's eyes widened. Her heart leaped into her throat and then immediately dropped to her toes.

This was the phone call she'd been waiting weeks to receive.

Pushing to her feet, she cut Asher a quick glance and

then walked away. She really didn't want him to hear her side of this conversation.

Crossing to the other side of the busy terminal, Kennedy tried to find a quiet corner.

"Hi, Simone. It's great to hear from you. I'm sorry about the noise, but I'm at the airport waiting to board a plane for work."

"Well then, I won't keep you. I just wanted to let you know that everyone at the firm was very impressed with your résumé and your Skype interview. If you're still interested, we'd like to offer you a position."

"Yes. Absolutely." She really needed to try a complete sentence. "I'm thrilled to get this opportunity."

Masters, Dillon and Cooper was one of the premier advertising agencies in the Pacific Northwest. They handled major corporate clients with ties in the area, including an international coffee chain, a well-known airline, an adventure vacation company and many more. This was the chance of a lifetime. Exactly the kind of position she'd envisioned when she'd chosen marketing as her major.

She'd been working her ass off the past five years to earn this kind of opportunity and couldn't believe she'd succeeded in landing it almost immediately after graduation.

Her hands started trembling, so much that Kennedy had to press the phone tight against her ear in order to hear the rest of what Simone said.

"Excellent. We're excited to have you on board. But we need you here in three weeks. Is that doable?"

Kennedy began pacing, her restless energy and excitement needing an outlet so she wouldn't squeal into the phone and scare the poor woman on the other end.

But that was a mistake, because when she turned, her gaze collided with Asher's from across the terminal. He was watching her, that intense stare sending another shot of adrenaline through her body.

His presence was a reminder of the hurdles she still had to jump in order to make this work.

"As I mentioned in my interview, I'm in the middle of a major project that I can't simply walk away from, but it should be complete by then."

"Excellent, because your start date is important. Mr. Masters, Ms. Dillon and Mr. Cooper are forming a new division of the company and plan to make you part of that team. The kickoff meeting is in three weeks, and they require everyone present then."

Kennedy swallowed, anxiety twisting in her belly. Three weeks wasn't a very long time to get her life ready to move across the country, especially when she would be spending the majority of that on a ship in the middle of the Caribbean. But this was too good an opportunity to pass up.

"That shouldn't be a problem."

"Wonderful. I'll send you an email with more details and some paperwork we'll need you to complete. Safe travels and we'll speak soon."

Kennedy murmured her goodbyes.

In an ideal world she'd have taken the time to make lists, sift through details and plan. But she was about to board a plane and then hop immediately onto a ship heading for the open sea. She didn't have the luxury of time.

And if making a handful of phone calls saved her the torture of sitting back down next to Asher, even better.

The first call she placed was to Jackson. He'd been

aware that she'd interviewed, but decided not to tell his business partners about her potential resignation until it was an actuality. Luckily, it was late afternoon where he was. Unfortunately, he didn't answer his phone, so she had to leave him a message. Not the way she wanted to break the news to him, but with the difference in their time zones and them both soon being in remote locations, she didn't have much choice.

The next call was to her parents, who were thrilled she'd gotten the position but upset she'd be leaving so soon. After sweet-talking her mom into some sorting and packing, Kennedy hung up the phone, still buzzing and giddy from the excitement.

Until she turned, her gaze landing on Asher once more and the blatant reminder that several things still had to fall into place.

No matter what happened, this documentary had to be completed on time if she had any hope of making it to Seattle.

2

IT HAD BEEN several months since he'd been on the *Amphitrite*, but he always enjoyed being out in the field. Asher pulled the sea air into his lungs, letting it fill him up. Warm sun beat down on his skin, reminding him just why he did this.

There was nothing like making your living with the beach as your office. Any beach. He'd seen some of the most gorgeous sites in the world…and some of the worst humanity had to offer.

But that was behind him, and something he'd never even think about changing. Serving with the SEALs had been an honor. A legacy. The best thing he could ever hope to do with his life.

He'd grown up with stories of his father, the hero. The flag they'd handed his grandmother across the casket had hung on the wall above his bed.

All things considered, his life had turned out pretty well…even if there were days he felt empty.

He might not have any real family—because it was difficult to think of his mom as family when he hadn't heard from her in twenty-seven years—but he didn't need any. He'd forged his own connections in the brotherhood he'd found with the SEALs and the two men he considered closer than friends. Jackson, Knox and the rest of the Trident team were all the family he needed.

The quiet shush of water against the hull of the ship worked to center him. A welcome distraction from the fiasco that was about to unfold.

It was late afternoon, the heavy orange-red sun hanging low against the horizon as they headed away from Nassau. It would take them several hours to reach the dive site. The team had come into port to get supplies and pick up Kennedy, himself and the production crew that had met them at the dock.

Asher had studiously avoided Kennedy and the pile of heavy black cases and bags that had been loaded on under her watchful eye. It was better for his peace of mind.

Unfortunately, her voice, sharp with censure, floated across the deck, making that difficult. "Be careful with that!"

He turned, slumping against the hard railing, arm outstretched across the smooth surface. His gaze followed her every move. She was a hard woman to ignore.

Kennedy was a whirlwind of action. She made him tired just watching. A tiny stick of dynamite. She was bossy, full of opinions and not hesitant about sharing them…with anyone and everyone. Honestly, she reminded him quite a lot of his grandmother.

He'd loved his grandma with all his heart. Had been devastated when she passed six years into his tour with the SEALs. She'd been tough and smart, sweet and exacting. She'd pushed him, often beyond the boundaries he thought he could reach.

But she'd loved him. In his entire life, his grandmother had been the only woman who ever had.

Kennedy was a princess, but not the annoying self-centered kind. It had taken him one family function with her brother and father both present to realize the men in her life had given her confidence, made her feel secure in herself and her place.

And that confidence looked good on her, even if it was occasionally intimidating.

She was barely five feet, but it was hard to remember that when she looked at you out of those whiskey-colored eyes, so warm and bright. He liked whiskey, especially on her.

Kennedy directed the group of people milling about. They reminded him of a colorful school of fish, darting here and there without any real direction. But he had no doubt she would bring order.

She instructed the production crew where to store their gear and what bunks they'd be occupying for the next few weeks. Without so much as a cheat sheet. Kennedy knew exactly who was who, where they belonged and kept all the shit straight in her head.

It was impressive.

And why she'd be so damn successful.

At first he'd been very vocal about his reluctance to hire Kennedy. She was young, still in college, and they'd been a fledgling company with enough things working against them. He'd wanted to hire someone with experience and contacts that could help get Trident Diving and Salvage established.

And then he'd met her. And his protests had doubled,

not because he thought she couldn't do the job—it had taken him five minutes to know that she could—but because he'd needed to put as much distance between them as possible for his sanity.

So he'd pushed in every way he could imagine, placing walls and anger and animosity between them, hoping they'd be insurmountable obstacles.

But somehow Kennedy always seemed to scale them.

About twenty minutes after they'd shoved off, the chaos abated. She stood on the now quiet deck, her feet spread wide to compensate for the motion of the ship. Asher had the perfect view of her ass and the tight denim shorts that cupped the curve of it. He wanted to run his palm up the bare skin of her thigh, slipping his fingers beneath the hem.

Biting back a curse, he watched her shoulders rise and fall on a heavy sigh. Her hands clenched into fists at her sides for several seconds before she unfurled them.

"Did you enjoy the show?" she finally asked, turning just enough to look at him across the slope of her shoulder.

He grinned. It shouldn't matter that she'd known he was there, watching. But it did.

"Always entertaining to watch you work, cupcake."

Her mouth tightened, and something dangerous flashed through her golden eyes before she got control of it again.

Turning deliberately, she faced him, letting her gaze slip across his body, taking in his negligent pose for several seconds before crossing the deck to him.

She stopped a couple of feet away, just out of reach. Smart woman.

Crossing her arms over her chest, Kennedy speared

him with a level gaze. "The crew would like to start tonight. Just a few test shots."

"Won't it be dark?"

Her lips twitched, drawing his attention. Part of him wanted to push until that ghost of a smile went full-blown, but he didn't. Because her smile was deadly.

"Did you notice all the crates? I'm pretty sure a few of them contained lighting equipment."

"S-Smart-ass." Asher ground his teeth together, forcing his mouth closed.

And there it was, what he'd been dreading from the moment Kennedy had backed him into a corner.

He waited for her to react, but she didn't. Instead, she shrugged. "They just want to get you on camera, no pressure and nothing important."

No pressure. That was a rich joke. This entire project was nothing but pressure. A situation he wasn't trained for and had zero experience handling. Hell, even thinking about it made his tongue swell, choking him—or at least if felt that way. It would get so much worse once the camera was in front of him, that blank eye staring, judging, recording every one of his failures for eternity.

And with Kennedy watching…all the ingredients for a full-blown disaster.

Her eyes ran up and down his body again. With one sweeping glance she ignited every nerve ending, making them all throb relentlessly.

He didn't want to want this woman. And, yet, he couldn't seem to stop his physical reactions to her— all of them.

"I'll have wardrobe come to your room in about an hour. You might want to take a shower."

Asher forced out a wicked grin. He chose his words carefully, deliberately. "You telling me I'm dirty, angel?"

She popped out a hip, balling a fist on it and glaring at him with irritation.

"Just so we're on the same page, are you planning on cooperating or making this whole experience a pain in my ass?"

He lifted a single eyebrow.

"Yeah, I know the question is stupid, but I had to ask." She let out a heavy sigh, closing her eyes for a few seconds. Suddenly, he could read all the little signs of exhaustion written into her face—the miniscule lines crinkling the corners of her mouth, the faint smudges of blue beneath her eyes, her drooping shoulders—and he wanted to fix it for her.

Shit.

"I have no intention of making your life difficult."

She laughed, the sound far from humorous. "We both know that isn't true, Ash. You delight in making my life difficult."

"Not this time."

"Yeah." She shook her head, the soft cloud of honey-blond hair swirling around her shoulders. He wanted to take a handful of it and run it through his fingers to see if it was as silky as it looked.

He wanted to walk away from her and the weakness she caused deep inside him. That's what he'd been doing for the past two years. Hell, that's what he'd done his entire life. But today there was nowhere left to go. They were stuck together on this ship, and Kennedy was about to become his shadow.

His body throbbed at the idea of her being so close.

Nope, not good. He couldn't want her. He couldn't touch her. She was Jackson's little sister, forbidden fruit.

Asher had no doubt what his friend's reaction would be if he ever touched Kennedy. Jackson was protective of his little sister, rightly so. He'd seen his friend put a fist through the face of a guy who had the misfortune of making a rather racy comment about Kennedy within Jackson's hearing. Poor bastard hadn't realized what had hit him until he was ass-down on the floor.

Jackson was family, but there was no question in Asher's mind who he would choose if forced to take sides.

And no woman, not even Kennedy, was worth losing the only family he had and the business he'd invested his entire future in.

"I'll believe that when I see it," she finally said, spinning away and leaving him standing alone on the deck.

KENNEDY STOOD OFF to the side, arms crossed over her chest as she watched the crew work. It was intriguing, her first shoot, although she had to admit she wasn't thrilled with the way Carmen, the makeup artist, was smiling and flirting with Asher. If she giggled one more time...

As if the man needed makeup to look gorgeous anyway. She had no doubt the camera was going to love him. Those mesmerizing eyes, sharp cheekbones and the tiny scar running right along the side of his lips... rakish, charming with the perfect dash of dangerous.

They'd commandeered the office. It was deep inside the belly of the ship, so a little darker than they'd wanted, but it provided a kind of professional setting the director was aiming for in these first shots, establishing Asher's experience and expertise before following him into the water.

She and Daniel, the director, were murmuring about the schedule when Asher's raised voice drifted up from the other side of the room.

"I'm not wearing that."

The sound of a chair scraping against the floor grated down Kennedy's spine.

Asher stood up, pulling out the paper towels Carmen had tucked into his collar to protect his dark navy T-shirt and threw them on the ground. "Kennedy!"

Everyone in the room turned to look at her. Dread and frustration spun in her belly. Beside her, the director stiffened. Biting back a curse, Kennedy narrowed her eyes, preparing for the explosion she could see coming.

The production company was already displeased that they were getting Asher instead of Jackson. She'd promised everyone involved that not only was Asher as knowledgeable about the *Chimera*, but that he'd be happy to cooperate with whatever they wanted to do.

So she'd basically lied, praying that she could keep control of the situation.

This outburst wasn't a good omen.

Spearing her with his gaze, Asher growled, "Get over here and fix this."

Throwing Daniel a tight-lipped smile, Kennedy excused herself and stalked over to where Asher stood in the corner of the room. The brunette with the brushes stared at them with wide eyes. The guy from wardrobe shifted on his feet, a suit—complete with matching vest and what appeared to be a bow tie—draped across his arms.

Asher lived in jeans, T-shirts, board shorts and flip-flops. He occasionally bowed to convention and put on a dress shirt and slacks for business meetings. She'd seen pictures of him in his military uniform and knew he must have worn formal dress on occasion. She remembered him wearing a suit once...but it definitely hadn't involved a vest and bow tie.

The thought of him with that brightly colored scrap of cloth tied around his neck had laughter bubbling up inside her throat. She tried to swallow it back but wasn't successful.

She took one look at Asher's angry expression and the wardrobe guy's hopeful gaze and knew this wouldn't end well.

"Tell him I'm not wearing this."

She shook her head. If she opened her mouth, she wasn't going to be able to keep the laughter in. And that would not help the situation at all.

Kennedy hadn't realized Daniel had followed her until his voice sounded behind her. "What's the problem?"

Crud, she needed to fix this before Asher opened his mouth and said something they'd all regret.

Better they think her crazy. Kennedy let the laughter she'd been holding back fill the space between them.

Every pair of eyes turned to her. Asher's eyebrows arrowed together, his mouth pulling down at the edges, making the white slash of his scar pop into sharp relief.

She held up a finger, pulled in a deep breath and was eternally grateful when everyone waited.

By the time she'd regained her composure, Asher had crossed his arms over his massive chest, biceps bulging. Damn the man was gorgeous.

Turning away, she directed her words to Cody, the

wardrobe guy. "Look, I get what you're trying to do. Does he look like a suit kind of guy? He spends most of his time wet and/or covered in sand."

"But surely..." Cody began, his words trailing off as he took in Asher standing like a forbidding Greek god.

"Why don't we compromise?" Turning to Asher, she continued, not giving anyone a chance to quash her plan. "Asher, I know for a fact this isn't the first time you've worn a suit."

"Baby girl, the last time I wore a suit like this was for my wedding. And the fact that my ex insisted should have been a clue the marriage was doomed."

Kennedy tried not to react to his words. She'd had no idea he'd been married. No one had mentioned it to her, although she supposed there really hadn't been a reason.

That little tease of information made her want to dig for more, but she pushed the urge away, trying to focus on the problem in front of her instead.

"One of the benefits of owning my own business is that I get to do what I want, which includes wearing whatever's comfortable. And that—" Asher pointed at the suit "—looks far from comfortable."

Daniel frowned and opened his mouth, but Kennedy cut him off. She really didn't want to know what he was going to say, because there was no way Asher would take it well.

"Surely we can come to some agreement. I have to admit, the bow tie is a bit much."

"It's trendy," Cody countered, his voice going up in defense of his choices.

"And might work with another man, but Asher Reynolds is an ex–navy SEAL. All the guys from Trident are. They aren't trendy. They're strong, dangerous, skilled.

You put him in that thing, and you're going to cover up what your viewers will fall in love with—his raw intensity and sexual charisma."

Turning away from Cody without giving him a chance to respond, Kennedy focused on Asher. "The slacks, the shirt. Sleeves rolled up and collar unbuttoned. Relaxed sophistication."

His eyes narrowed. She silently pleaded with him, unsure whether or not it would make a damn bit of difference.

Everyone stood there, silent, as tension stretched out second by second.

"No jacket and no goddamn vest."

Kennedy nodded her head, relief flooding her. Grabbing the clothes from Cody, she shoved them into Asher's arms before he changed his mind. "Go, put these on."

He disappeared down the hall. The noise inside the room, which really wasn't big enough to hold all the people and camera equipment, gradually increased to a normal level, or what she was coming to realize was normal for a functioning set.

But it all fell off again several minutes later. Kennedy, talking with the set director about moving some things off the desk, looked around and nearly swallowed her tongue.

Asher stood in the open doorway, a frown pulling at his lips as he fiddled with one of his cuffs. Damn, the man should wear a suit more often.

The snow-white shirt was crisp and made his tanned skin pop. The pants, a dark gray with a faint black pinstripe, hugged his hips and strained against the massive circumference of his thighs.

Beside her, she heard a soft voice whisper, "You were so right." Glancing over, she took in Carmen, her beautiful blue eyes full of hero worship.

That propelled Kennedy forward, although she had no idea why.

Taking Asher's arm, she pulled him across the room and over to the desk. The production team had debated having him sit in the chair behind the desk, but with the more casual wardrobe choice, they'd agreed to try it with him leaning against the edge, ankles crossed. As if he was talking to a buddy.

It had taken everything inside Kennedy for her to bite her tongue during the discussion. They hadn't wanted her opinion, even if she did have a freakin' marketing degree with a keen eye for composition and graphic design.

Putting her hands on his hips, she pushed Asher backward until his body folded.

"Wh-what are you doing?" he asked, his eyes narrowed and his entire body tight.

"Putting you where I want you," she said, glancing up through her lashes for a second before jerking her gaze back down. Bad idea. Studying Asher Reynolds was like looking directly at a solar eclipse, likely to blind you. And she couldn't afford that right now.

She waited for the rude comeback—she'd given him a perfect setup—but none followed.

Grasping the cuff he'd been fiddling with, she pulled it back down and smoothed the edges out before folding it into place. The backs of her fingers brushed against his warm skin. His soft arm hair tickled her nerve endings. He flexed, the muscles along his arm bulging.

Had he done that on purpose?

Satisfied with his cuff, Kennedy stepped back. She let her gaze run up him, trying to be objective. This was just like any other product she'd ever marketed. Color, composition, impact, message.

There were things about working at Trident that she absolutely loved. But the thrill of using her skills—of doing what she enjoyed and was good at—effervesced through her body. Working for a diving company just didn't give her enough opportunities to use her training.

Asher looked elegantly casual. As if he'd just spent hours working a major business deal and finally had a chance to relax.

There was just one thing wrong…

Stepping back to him, Kennedy went up on her tip-toes. She was short and he was tall. Even with Asher leaning against the desk, she couldn't reach what she wanted without pressing her entire body against him.

She tried not to notice the way her breasts brushed the hard plane of his chest as she dug her fingers into his hair.

Asher shifted beneath her. His hands landed on her hips. She felt the heat of them down to her toes.

"What are you doing?"

Kennedy didn't answer but ran her fingers through his hair, rumpling the light brown strands. Whoever had done it had obviously been going for a more formal look, which might have worked before but not now. They'd slicked through a bunch of gel, trying to tame the natural wave his hair had when it grew a little too long.

She liked the waves. They were rakish and fit his personality. She fussed and tugged, prolonging the contact a few seconds more than necessary. Yeah, so she was human.

Finally forcing herself to push away from him, Kennedy tried to ignore the way his hands lingered for several seconds.

"Better," she said, her voice suddenly scratchy.

Clearing her throat, Kennedy tried to find her professionalism. She knew it was inside, buried deep. And she needed it. Right now.

Turning away, she gestured to the director. "He's all yours."

3

His HEAD WAS so scrambled. Having Kennedy pressed against his body, her hands threading through his hair as her fingernails gently scraped against his scalp had been heaven. And torture.

Thank God no one seemed to notice the heavy bulge behind the zipper of his pants.

All around him there was a whirlwind of activity. People speaking to each other as if he wasn't even there. The woman with the makeup brushes just walked up and started messing with his face without even giving him a heads-up.

The tech guys spoke back and forth in a language that sounded like something foreign, even though he was certain they were speaking English. He had no idea what a gyro camera was, but apparently it was supposed to counter the constant motion of the ship as they filmed.

Kennedy and Daniel had their heads together. She fit right in. The gleam of excitement in her eyes and slight flush to her cheeks were difficult to miss. She was enjoying this while he was fighting the urge to vomit.

The familiar helplessness churned in his belly. That fear and anxiety crawling up his skin, making it burn. If he thought there was any chance at all to get Kennedy banished from this room he would have done it. The cameras were going to be bad enough, but with her there… Asher wasn't sure he'd be able to hold it together.

But just watching her, he knew nothing short of a hurricane would force her out of this room right now.

She'd spent months putting this project together. It meant everything to her.

Kennedy was completely oblivious to the effect she had on people. Which only made her more dangerous.

She wasn't perfect. By the end of the day her makeup was often smudged, just enough to make her look adorable. When it was free, her hair usually rained down her back in reckless waves that refused to be tamed. And when she tried tying it into a knot on top of her head, pieces always escaped to curl against her neck and cheeks.

Like now.

Instead of using an elastic band like a normal woman, she'd found a couple of pens and stuck them in like sticks to hold the messy coil on her head.

"All right." Daniel clapped his hands. The room went silent, everyone stopping what they were doing.

"We're going to take our time here, folks. Asher is new to being in front of the camera, although Kennedy assures me he's a natural."

A natural. Jesus, could she have told a bigger lie?

Daniel smiled at Kennedy. Asher had no idea how she'd managed it, but the man's earlier irritation had disappeared. Kennedy grinned back at him, her enthusiasm glittering and contagious.

For a minute he wanted to believe everything was going to be okay.

And then his gaze swung to the empty eye of the camera and panic seized him.

His tongue swelled. His chest tightened, one pound of pressure adding to two and then more, as if he'd gone fast beneath the waves without taking the time to pressurize. The heaviness settled deep, pressing on his lungs and making it difficult to pull in a full breath.

Closing his eyes, Asher tried to find a center of calm, but all he got was a memory of his mother. Her expression full of impatience, anger and disappointment. As if he'd been a reminder of everything that was wrong with her life.

He'd been young when she left, just six. Those were the only memories he really had of the woman, her presence in his life limited even before his father had died and she'd abandoned him for good.

Asher forcibly pushed the memories away. It had been years since his mother had invaded his thoughts, and he didn't like her there. It bothered him that he'd let her in, especially when he was already fighting to keep his cool.

He remembered nights out in harsh environments with only the supplies he could carry and the men beside him standing against death and disaster. He hadn't felt this kind of panic then, not even when they'd been ambushed, lost communications with their evac team and spent hours trading gunfire and trying to figure out an exit strategy.

"Asher." Kennedy's soft voice pulled him out of the

mental tailspin. His gaze snapped to hers, zeroing in on those warm brown eyes. "Daniel wants you to just talk a bit about the *Chimera*. How did Trident get involved with hunting for the ship? Go into a bit about how you, Jackson and Knox met."

Asher clung desperately to the excuse she'd given him. "You know I can't talk about our missions with the SEALs."

She shook her head. "That's not what I mean. Or not exactly. Just…how did you guys become friends, start the business?"

"All right."

Asher took a deep breath. With Kennedy close, he suddenly felt as if he was going to suffocate sitting in this tiny room.

She frowned at him, creases forming right between her eyes. He could imagine the disappointment that would fill them when she finally realized he was about to ruin everything.

"Are you okay?"

"Fine," he gritted out, not meaning it at all. But he wasn't about to tell her the truth.

Her whiskey eyes toured his face. Years of practice allowed Asher to clamp down on his reactions, forcing a calm he didn't feel to settle over his features.

Her mouth compressed into a tight line, but before she could say anything more, Daniel squeezed between them.

"Kennedy has explained what I'm looking for?"

"Yes," Asher answered, forcefully pulling his gaze away from Kennedy.

"Excellent."

Everyone backed away from him, and for the first

time since walking into the room, his personal space was his own. He'd wanted that, but the relief was short-lived when the people who'd crowded in scuttled off to the edges of the room.

They were lined up against the wall, out of the line of the camera, but available should they be needed.

And they were all staring at him. Silent. Waiting.

He'd lived through this nightmare before. Sitting in the middle of a classroom with all the kids around him playing witness to his humiliation and failure. Impatience oozing from them because he couldn't open his mouth and get a simple goddamn word past his unco-operative vocal cords to answer the teacher.

The frustration and resentment.

But this was different than those moments. So much worse. Everything he said and did would not only be witnessed by these people, but recorded and reflected back. Every flaw and gaffe magnified for the entire world to see.

He'd faced down terrorists, bombers—men, women and, hell, children—who'd wanted to kill him merely because of who he was and what he represented. With the SEALs he'd gained a reputation for having ice in his veins, walking into the most chaotic situations with a confidence that bordered on insanity.

Because he trusted in his training, his skills and those of the men fighting beside him.

It was terrifying not to be able to trust his own body to perform the way it should. Not to have the skills to conquer the irrational fear roiling inside of him because of a stupid inanimate object—a camera.

He would not lose his shit now. Not over this.

Swallowing the gigantic lump that was trying to suffocate him, Asher's gaze found the expectant eye of the lens…and Kennedy. She stood several feet behind the camera positioned on the large metal frame.

To her left the director said, "Action."

To her right the camera moved. Asher's system flooded with adrenaline. His senses, dialed up to a ten already, kicked into overdrive.

His fingers curled around the edge of the desk, the wood biting into his skin hard enough to leave marks.

His mouth opened, but nothing came out.

The director cut a glance at Kennedy, who frowned and shifted uncomfortably on her feet.

"Asher, why don't you start by telling us who you are and how you got involved with Trident Diving?"

He nodded, swallowed and tried again. But nothing came out.

Shit.

The quiet that had descended over the room began to fade. Feet shuffled. Someone murmured. Somewhere paper fluttered.

He wasn't going to be able to do this.

The memory of every humiliation he'd ever experienced because of his failures came flooding back to him. His struggle to be understood through the debilitating stutter that all the experts claimed was psychological, but that he couldn't seem to stop. Each time he'd seen sorrow, frustration and disappointment in his grandmother's eyes when therapy didn't work. His inability to make his mom happy. Make her stay. Walking into his home, after being gone for months, to find it absolutely empty of everything but the divorce papers Krista had left for him.

"Fuck this," he growled, shoving away from the desk

and stalking toward the door. He didn't need to add another failure to a list that was already plenty long.

No one tried to stop him. The crowd stared even as they parted to let him pass. He didn't look at any of them.

He didn't need to.

The expression of utter horror on Kennedy's face was enough.

HOLY HELL, WHAT had just happened?

One minute Asher had been leaning against the desk looking all remote, brooding and eminently lickable, and the next he'd been cursing and storming out.

The second he disappeared every eye in the place turned to her. She had no clue what to say.

Daniel scowled at her. "What was that?"

She shook her head, at a complete loss. "I have no idea."

"Ms. Duchane, I'm sure I don't need to tell you how valuable our time is. Every minute we sit idle costs the company money. No one is going to be happy about this. Our entire show revolves around that man." He pointed out the door.

"I'll fix this."

"You better. No one at Naughton Media was thrilled when your brother backed out."

Yeah, neither was she, but there wasn't much she could do about it.

"I have just as much invested in this as you do, Daniel." Maybe more since her entire future hinged on this going well. If the documentary faltered her position in Seattle could be in jeopardy.

Kennedy pulled in some much-needed oxygen, hoping it would settle her own jangling nerves.

"Look, I just need a little time to figure out what's going on." Turning fully toward him, she placed her hand on his arm and pressed into his personal space. It was a calculated tactic, but one she didn't feel a smidge of remorse for employing.

She'd do whatever she had to in order to fix this.

"It isn't like you can just pack up and leave."

She realized maybe those weren't the best words she could have chosen when Daniel's mouth went tight.

"I'll take care of it," she promised again.

She didn't wait for Daniel to react before pushing through the people clustered at the doorway.

She stood in the hallway for several seconds, scrolling through a list of places in her head that Asher could have disappeared to. His room was a logical choice, but he'd realize that and probably avoid it. There was the upper deck, but it wouldn't provide much in the way of privacy. The captain was in the wheelhouse steering the *Amphitrite*. The galley and mess were rejected pretty much before she'd thought of them because everyone went there when they had time off.

Where would he go?

In a flash, it hit her. When Jackson was frustrated, he turned to the water. When Knox needed to clear his head, he took his car out on to the open road. On more than one occasion she'd found Asher in an empty office at Trident, the guts of several guns spread out across the desk as he painstakingly cleaned each one.

The only problem was empty space was at a premium. Luckily, she knew a little secret.

Instead of heading toward the open deck, Kennedy

strode farther down the hall, away from the fresh air and light. Down a tight set of stairs at the back of the hallway.

The noise of the engines rumbled louder and louder, but she ignored it. The vibration running through her chest was more difficult to dismiss.

The space was dark and damp and uncomfortably warm from the combination of tropical heat and running engines. Her clothes began to cling to her skin.

There was a small room that most people didn't even know was down here. They stored spare parts for the ship, tools, equipment that was rarely used.

And a small table she'd never understood the need for. She did now.

Jerking open the door, she was pleased when her hunch proved correct. Asher didn't even look up as he continued to break apart the piece in his hands.

She couldn't help but watch his dexterous fingers sliding across the smooth metal with authority and familiarity.

What would those hands feel like on her skin?

Kennedy pushed the question away, refusing to acknowledge that it even existed.

"What the hell happened back there?" she asked.

His hot gaze flicked up to hers for a brief moment before dropping back to his task.

At least he didn't try to pretend he had no clue what she was talking about…he simply ignored her. Kennedy thought maybe that was worse.

Her temper flared, which wasn't anything new with this man. There was something about Asher that got under her skin, pulled a reaction from her that seemed too big to control.

What was it about him that drew her in even as she realized the only result would be pain, irritation and probably humiliation?

Today, she'd had enough.

Stalking forward, Kennedy stopped on the opposite side of the table from him. Without hesitation, she leaned over and snatched the gun out of his hand.

He reached after her, trying to grab it back. She might be small, but she was quick, and the table stood between them.

"Give that back," he growled. "You could hurt yourself."

"Please." To prove her point, Kennedy studied the weapon for a moment, scooped up the missing parts from the table and quickly reassembled the piece.

She had to admit, his stunned, slack-jawed expression left her feeling rather smug.

"Do you really think my brother would let his little sister go without marksman lessons? I've been going to the shooting range with my dad and Jackson since I was in pigtails. I know my way around a weapon, soldier."

For the first time in their abbreviated history, Kennedy felt as if she had Asher off-kilter. It was a heady experience. One that made her a little bolder than she normally would have been.

Skirting around the table, she stepped closer to him. She blindly set the gun on the flat surface behind her.

"Now that we have the distractions out of the way, why don't you tell me what's going on?"

His bright green eyes flashed, reminding her of cool spring forests and the scent of pine needles crushed underfoot. "The distractions are far from out of the way."

For a second she thought his gaze caught and held

on her mouth. But that couldn't be right. And he obviously hadn't meant his words the way her libido wanted to take them.

Maybe this was a bad idea. Her brain told her she needed to turn away and walk out the door. But she didn't. Couldn't. Kennedy stared up at him, her throat tight and heart hammering against her ribs for some unfathomable reason.

She wasn't scared. She wasn't even angry, not really. But her entire body was energized. Alive.

She always felt this way around Asher. It was exhilarating, not to mention exceedingly frustrating, considering on most days she wasn't even certain she liked the man. Apparently, her body didn't seem to care.

At his sides, Asher's fingers flexed, curling into tight fists before relaxing and curling again.

"Ash," she said in a calm, even voice. "I'm here to help, but I can't do that if you're not straight with me."

He looked away. The edge of his jaw ticked.

"I told you already I can't do this."

She laughed. She didn't mean to, but it escaped before she could help herself.

"This isn't f-funny," he growled.

No, she didn't think it was, either. "You're one of the most capable men I've ever met, Asher. It's no secret that you and I rub each other the wrong way."

His fists flexed again, his body looming a little closer.

"But that doesn't mean I'm blind or can't appreciate what you bring to the team. I honestly don't think there's any problem you couldn't tackle. Anyone you couldn't charm. You're abrasive and irreverent, but even that can be endearing because it means you're honest and forthright."

Her own words were revving the exasperation simmering beneath her surface. Why the hell was he balking?

"So, I'm basically calling bullshit. You can do this. You just don't want to, and I can't for the life of me understand why."

Asher stood inches away from her. He towered above her, those damn green eyes drilling deep inside her with an intensity that made her belly flutter.

"I have a problem." Each word was clipped and deliberate, almost as if he was grinding them out like broken glass between his clenched teeth.

"Obviously. Why don't you tell me what it is, so I can fix it?"

He shook his head.

She growled beneath her breath.

Asher glared at her for several seconds, the burden of their mingled frustration a physical weight pressing in on them both.

His lips drew tight, flattening into a harsh line. It didn't take a genius to realize he wanted her to leave. Tough. She wasn't going anywhere until this was solved.

"I don't like being on camera. I have a st-st-stutter that gets worse when I'm under stress. Starring in your damn documentary pretty much pulls every trigger. I can't do it."

Kennedy's eyes widened. She took in Asher's grim expression. The way his shoulders had begun to hunch downward. She'd watched this man storm into their conference room. She'd seen him chew out one of the guys on their dive team because he'd been lax about his safety procedures. On several nights out with the team after work, she'd watched him deliberately, coolly and expertly seduce some bar bunny into going home with him.

For a brief moment she wanted to laugh again. But she couldn't. Because she'd heard the hesitation in his words.

It wasn't the first time she'd heard it, either, but it was the first time she'd really thought about it. It didn't happen often.

She'd listened as he'd addressed boardrooms, led conference calls and shot the shit with her brother and Knox countless times without the hint of a problem.

In fact, in all the time she'd known him, she could count on one hand the number of times it had happened. Before, she'd dismissed it. Hell, sometimes her brain moved faster than her mouth and she stumbled over words.

But his scant flash of horror, concealed almost before it had a chance to appear, made her pause for the briefest moment.

Slowly, she said, "Okay."

Her heart thumped erratically inside her chest. He hid it well, but Kennedy could see the edge of vulnerability that Asher's admission had cost him. Could see the tension filling his body as he braced for her to verbally pounce on what he'd just revealed.

Because that was the relationship they'd shared for months.

But this wasn't him ribbing her about the night he'd bailed her out of jail for indecent exposure or her teasing him about the revolving door he'd clearly installed in his bedroom.

One long look into his brilliant green eyes and her chest ached for him.

Damn the man for actually being human.

An expletive ran through her head. Kennedy's knees buckled. Luckily, she was close enough to the table that her rear hit the edge instead of the floor.

Asher's hands bracketed her hips, steadying her. "Easy."

The imprint of each of his fingers burned into her skin. Kennedy registered her body's reaction to his touch but pushed it aside. She didn't want to notice how he made her feel. And she had bigger fish to fry.

Oh, this was a clusterfuck of immeasurable proportions.

"Why didn't you tell me before now?" she finally whispered. If he'd been honest with her, she might have been able to find a way to fix this mess. Now they were both stuck in the middle of the Caribbean with a production team that expected a beautiful former navy SEAL as an expert, and she had none.

"Right, because there's nothing humiliating about admitting that kind of weakness to a beautiful woman."

Kennedy wasn't sure which part of that statement to address first.

"But I'm not some woman, Asher. We're colleagues. You're my brother's business partner and friend. What did you think I would do?"

He shrugged, looking wholly vulnerable and adorable all at once. It was unexpected and called to the quiet place inside her that liked being needed.

"I haven't exactly made your life easy."

"Jesus, Ash, we snipe at each other, like siblings."

His fingers slipped beneath the hem of her shirt,

grazing the bare skin at her hip. She couldn't stop the involuntary inhalation of surprise that whistled past her parted lips.

Asher groaned. "Not like siblings."

What the hell was going on? Had she walked through that door and into an alternate universe?

No, this couldn't be happening. Not now. She'd ignored her attraction to Asher for two years. Gone out of her way to subvert it.

Given her sketchy history with men, the last thing she needed was to get entangled with her brother's business partner and best friend. Not to mention a man who was technically her boss.

Placing her hands on Asher's chest, Kennedy pushed. For several seconds, he resisted, an immovable wall of male flesh that made her feel itchy and needy and trapped all at once. Until he stepped back and cool air flooded her lungs.

"So," Kennedy said, forcing determination and a calm she didn't quite feel into her voice. "What are we going to do?"

4

WHAT WERE THEY going to do? *They* weren't going to do anything. He was going to have to figure his way out of this one.

But the first thing he needed to do was get Kennedy out of here. He'd been in some of the most remote, desolate and hot as hell places on earth. But with her standing so close to him, Asher felt as if the air was an inch thick, clogging his lungs. That damn scent of hers clung to him, something sweet with an undercurrent of spice. A little innocent and a lot tempting.

"*We* aren't going to do anything, cupcake." He frowned, pulling his focus away from her and onto the gun sitting on the table behind her.

She'd shocked the hell out of him, putting that Beretta together so quickly.

He wasn't the kind of man who thought women couldn't do things like that. He'd worked with plenty of women in the service who were just as fierce and capable as their male counterparts. It had simply surprised him when Kennedy had done it.

He'd never seen her at the shooting range and didn't realize she had the skills.

He was impressed.

And didn't want to be.

Krista had always turned her nose up whenever he brought out his weapons. She'd complained that he spent money on them. It bothered her when he went to the range to practice. It never seemed to register with her that the skills he was honing kept him alive and brought him home to her every time he walked out the door.

The gun safe was one of the few things she'd left when she'd cleaned out their house.

Kennedy crossed her arms over her chest. This up close and personal it was difficult to ignore the way her breasts rounded higher, pressing against the tight confines of her shirt.

The erection he'd been sporting earlier roared back to life, pounding incessantly behind his zipper.

"The next time you call me cupcake, I'm going to shove one in your face. Fair warning. And if you think I'm going to just walk away from this and pretend everything's okay, you have another think coming. This is my project, Asher. My job. Work with me here."

She wasn't going to leave this alone. He'd known Kennedy long enough to realize that when she sank her teeth into a problem, she didn't let go until it was solved. Her single-minded determination was both frustrating and admirable.

Nothing stood in her way. In some ways, Kennedy reminded him of his grandmother. That woman hadn't pulled any punches, literally. She'd been a true Southern matriarch, willing to cuff him upside the head for being disrespectful, only to follow up the deserved pun-ishment with the warmest, biggest hug on the planet.

She'd never hesitated to put him in his place when he'd needed it, and as an angry, scared, hurting adoles-cent, he'd needed it often. She'd had the highest hopes for him, expecting him to do her and the memory of his father proud.

When his father was killed in action and his mother abandoned him, his grandmother had given him a safe place. So he'd wanted desperately to make her proud. His every decision growing up had been for that one purpose.

But the pressure he'd felt to live up to the glowing ideal of his father and make up for his mother dump-ing him on her doorstep had been huge. Difficult for a child to shoulder.

Right now, he felt the same weight as Kennedy stared up at him expectantly.

"I've got this," Asher forced out.

"Obviously not, or you wouldn't have run from that room like someone had tossed in a grenade."

Kennedy pressed closer. Asher countered with a sin-gle step backward. He would have gone farther, but his back collided with the solid plane of the wall. Damn the small room.

She crowded him, glaring up out of those mesmer-izing eyes, golden and fierce.

"You're not going to g-give up on this, are you?"

"No."

He stared down at her, his mind spinning and his body in turmoil—his need for her intertwining uncom-fortably with the fear that surfaced each time he thought about standing in front of those damn cameras.

"Fine. Then why don't you come up with a solution to a problem I've been dealing with since I was six." Asher crossed his arms over his chest, placing a physical barrier between them.

Her mouth opened and then shut. She stared up at him. Asher could practically see the wheels turning behind her eyes. God, he loved watching her mind work. She was observant and intuitive. She was good with people, which was a skill he'd had to fight tooth and nail to develop.

Her lush lips tightened. Her shoulders straightened. And tiny grooves crinkled the spot right between her eyes as she gave him a little frown. "I'm sorry, Asher. I didn't mean to imply that you couldn't handle the problem."

"Oh, I think you did. I get that this project is important to you. But I'm the one in f-f-front of the camera."

She shifted, resting a soft hand on his arm. The heat of her palm soaked through the thin layer of the dress shirt, sending a zing of need ripping straight through him.

"Okay, so the cameras make you nervous?"

"The cameras. The people. The idea of stuttering in front of an audience. I don't know what I'm doing, Kennedy, and stress makes the stutter worse."

"I've seen you in stressful situations before without any sign of a stutter."

"Sure, because I was trained and prepared, knew I could handle things. I'm not ready for this."

A smile bloomed across Kennedy's face.

Asher blinked, unable to look away. Kennedy was gorgeous in a girl-next-door kind of way. But when she smiled, true happiness or excitement shining from those tempting golden eyes…there was nothing more appealing.

"I think I have an idea." She cocked her head to the side. "I'm going to see if I can work some magic. Meet me in my room in an hour."

She turned to leave but paused just inside the doorway, her eyes raking over him from head to toe. Every molecule in his body felt the weight of her gaze.

"Leave the shirt and slacks on."

And then she was gone.

KENNEDY WAS OUT of her element, but that didn't faze her. She'd figure it out.

Hunting down one of the cameramen, Neil, she hauled him off to a quiet corner of the ship.

"I need to borrow your camera."

He blinked. "Uh…what?"

"I need to borrow your camera."

"Not just no, but, hell no."

Kennedy wasn't stupid. She'd known it would take some cajoling to get what she wanted. She'd once been told her brother was a brilliant strategist. She wasn't so bad herself.

Glancing down, she sauntered closer, tipped her lips into a sultry smile and then looked up at Neil through her lashes.

"Neil, do you like your job?"

The man was young, probably only a couple of years older than she was. A junior member of the team. Someone she'd immediately picked out as a weak link.

"Yes."

"Well, so do I. We have a problem. I'm trying to fix

it. But in order to do that, I need to borrow your camera."

"It's an expensive piece of equipment, Kennedy. If I give it to you and something happens, I'm responsible for it."

"No, you're not. First, I won't let anything happen. Second, if something does, I'll accept responsibility, and Trident will cover the cost of the camera."

Neil swallowed hard. "Okay."

She gathered the equipment she needed, grateful for the semester she'd worked as an intern at the local TV station.

The camera was only a foot or so in length and light enough to be handheld, with a large fuzzy mic protruding out the far end. It was portable, although she set it up on a tripod in the corner of her room. She needed the camera running but didn't have enough hands to operate it.

The rest of the time she spent with her fingers flying over the keyboard of her laptop as she took a crash course in everything she could find on stuttering.

They had a problem; she was going to solve it. Because this project could not get delayed. Not when Seattle was the pot of gold at the end of the rainbow.

A little over an hour later, she had a plan of action. Distraction seemed to be a key component for stuttering therapy. Stutterers often found that their issue became a self-fulfilling prophecy. High-pressure situations made them worry about stuttering, which often led to an increased occurrence of the stutter. Based on what Asher had told her, that sounded exactly like what he was experiencing.

She was fiddling with the camera, making sure

all the wires were connected correctly, when a voice sounded behind her.

"What's all that?"

Kennedy let out a startled squeak and jumped, spinning to find Asher standing next to her bed. She hadn't even heard him come in.

"A camera."

He'd left the clothes on as she'd instructed, and she was struck again by just how amazing he looked.

"I can see that. Why?"

Shoving his hands into the pockets of his slacks, he rocked back on his heels.

"We're going to put you in front of it and see if we can figure out something that'll help you get through the next couple weeks."

Kennedy turned away, continuing to fiddle as she spoke to him over her shoulder. "I thought a session with just me and the camera might help you feel more comfortable tomorrow, take away some of the stress so you're less likely to stutter."

Satisfied everything was working, she turned back to Asher and stopped dead in her tracks.

With nowhere else to sit, he'd chosen her bed. But he hadn't been content with perching on the edge. Nope. At some point he'd toed off his shoes and sprawled out, making himself completely at home. Propped up on one elbow, there was something wicked and unapologetic about the way he gazed at her like a lover waiting patiently for her to rejoin him in bliss.

Kennedy cleared her throat.

His arm bulged against the rolled shirt cuff. The fabric gaped against the tanned skin of his chest, giving her a little glimpse of his muscled pecs beneath the starched cotton.

Nope. She wasn't going there. Forcing her gaze away, she grumbled, "Sit up," smacking at his leg to make her point.

Moving back behind the camera, she focused it. Asher in all his masculine, larger-than-life, charismatic glory filled the small screen in front of her face.

She hit Record, watching as a red light blinked several times before going solid.

Not only had Asher ignored her direction, he'd rolled over on to his back and was staring at the ceiling.

Kennedy opened her mouth to argue with him, but shut it before she could say anything. If that was the first step he needed, then she'd give it to him. They had to start somewhere.

"What do you want me to d-do?" he asked, directing his question to the ceiling.

Kennedy could feel the gentle sway of the ship beneath her spread feet. Hear the distant hum of the engine as it vibrated through the room. Somehow the normal background noise made Asher's reluctance even more pronounced.

"Talk," she finally answered.

"About what?"

"I don't care. Trident. Your dog. The last woman you screwed." Oops, she hadn't meant to say that one out loud.

Twisting his head, Asher glared at her. "Not funny, Kennedy."

She shrugged, trying to brush it off as a joke. "Whatever takes your mind off the camera."

He turned his head again, bringing his focus up. "I

don't have a dog, something you already know. You could probably speak more intelligently about Trident than I could."

Which wasn't true, but since those were easily the most words he'd said to her at one time without glaring or following up with some smart-ass remark, she wasn't going to interrupt him to say so.

"And I'm not touching the last one with a ten foot pole."

"Oh, come on. I've heard you with the guys. You have no problem giving Jackson and Knox a blow-by-blow—pun obviously intended—account of your conquests."

A smirk tugged at the edges of his lips. Kennedy took a couple of steps sideways, wanting to see his expression better.

"Have you been eavesdropping, naughty little g-girl?"

She scoffed, the harsh sound scraping through her throat. "It can't be considered eavesdropping when you make zero attempt at keeping the conversation private. Naughty? Yes. Little girl? Not in a very long time."

His deep green gaze found hers, sending an unwanted shiver racing down her spine. "I remember," he drawled, pulling the syllables out in that slow, sexy way of his.

His voice was lethal, even with the stutter. Maybe especially with the stutter. It made him endearing, a word she never would have used to describe him.

"How long did it take you to get rid of the idiot who got you arrested, anyway? I never asked."

"About twenty minutes after you bailed me out of jail."

He grunted, a sound she took as approval. Not a difficult mental leap to make, considering he'd been pissed that she let the asshole talk her into something so stupid. The car ride home that night had been humiliating and uncomfortable. Asher had glared at her, silently judging even as he'd refused to yell at her as she knew he'd wanted to.

If he had, maybe their entire relationship would have been different. Maybe she wouldn't have felt so guilty and ashamed around him.

"It wasn't entirely his fault."

"On that we both agree. What in God's name possessed you to get naked on a park slide in the middle of the night?"

Kennedy felt her skin go hot. She normally wasn't the kind of woman to get embarrassed. Her parents had instilled in her a healthy sense of self-esteem. Her actions and decisions were her business, and there were only a handful of people whose opinions mattered to her. Unfortunately, Asher seemed to be one of them.

"Hormones?"

Getting arrested for indecent exposure had been the most embarrassing experience of her life…and of course Asher had been there to witness the aftermath.

Jackson had only been home for a few weeks at that point, bringing Asher and Knox with him to begin the process of opening a new business.

That night, a guy she'd met at a party had coaxed her into doing something spontaneous and daring. Stupid.

Thanks to an abundance of alcohol, she'd been pretty uninhibited, right up until the cops arrived, and the self-righteous coward had fled, leaving her half-naked and alone to be carted off to jail.

Her humiliation had been complete when she'd

walked down the hallway of the jail to see Asher waiting for her on the other side of the locked door.

He'd been pissed, his jaw drawn so tight she could see a muscle ticking there from several feet away. He hadn't said anything. The way he'd glared at her out of those flashing green eyes had been enough to send her stomach somersaulting.

And she hadn't much appreciated it. She'd already been emotionally raw, and Asher's silent judgment hadn't helped.

She'd also been bedraggled, exhausted and scared. Not her finest hour.

Shaking her head, Kennedy realized they needed to move off this subject…especially since it was on camera and she'd successfully hidden her one stint in jail from her parents and brother. Somehow, Asher had gotten the charges dropped. She'd never asked him how. Actually, she'd never thanked him. Because she hadn't realized he'd done it until days later.

"Thanks, by the way."

"For what?"

"Taking care of the charges."

He shrugged, stacking his hands behind his head and shifting to get a better view of her. "Not a big deal."

"It was to me. And for keeping the incident to yourself. Most guys would have gone running to my brother."

"Please. Jackson's in no position to cast stones. He's made plenty of boneheaded decisions in his life, and I was present for more than half of them. Hell, I even talked him into a few of them."

She laughed, the tension that had filled her body slowly leaking out. This was nice. Something she really hadn't experienced with Asher before. From that night going forward, there'd been this wall of antagonism sitting between them. But tonight, it was gone, replaced by something a heck of a lot more dangerous.

Slipping onto the edge of the bed, Kennedy folded her legs beneath her. "You'll have to tell me some of those stories."

"I don't think so, cupcake."

Part of her wanted to growl at him for using the derogatory nickname again, only this time when he said it, it didn't sound like a curse, but a caress.

And she wasn't going to push. Not when he'd been talking for five minutes with the camera rolling and no sign of a stutter.

"So, tell me something else. What were you like as a kid?"

He stiffened. Kennedy didn't understand his reaction, but before she could ask, every muscle in his body relaxed again, as if on cue.

"I grew up with my grandma. She raised me after my dad was killed in Iraq, in the same house he grew up in. I slept in his old room, played with the toys she'd saved."

Kennedy had no idea how to react to that.

"Wasn't that…kind of heavy? I mean, a constant reminder of what you'd lost."

"No, it made me feel closer to him."

Kennedy wanted to change the subject, partly because this wasn't where she'd expected the conversation to go. But mostly because she was too interested. She didn't need to think of Asher as a grief-stricken little boy.

She didn't need to be thinking about him at all. And, yet… "I'm guessing you were a hellion."

He flashed her that wicked grin, the one that made her go weak in the knees whenever he aimed it in her direction.

"Are you kidding me? My grandma wouldn't allow me to be a hellion. Although, my teenage years were a little harrowing for both of us. It was difficult not having a male figure in my life. Luckily, I had coaches and teachers who tried to fill the void as much as possible. When I'd let them."

Kennedy rolled her shoulders, realizing for the first time just how much strain had settled there. The past few days had been hectic. Hell, the past few weeks had been stressful as she'd worked to pull all the pieces together for this project and interview for the position in Seattle.

Reaching up over her head, she tried to work out a kink.

"What's wrong?"

"Nothing."

Asher grumbled beneath his breath. She couldn't hear all the words but caught enough to realize he was bashing all women who employed the word *nothing* when it obviously didn't apply.

"Fine. I think I pulled something carrying the camera equipment. It'll be okay. I just need to loosen it up."

"Come here," Asher said, shifting his body until he was propped up against the wall at the head of the bed.

"What?"

Motioning her closer, he repeated, "Come here."

She eyed him. "Why? What are you going to do?"

"Jeez, just do as you're told."

She laughed. "Not likely."

That smirk was back, a wicked little tilt to his lips

that matched the impish glint in his eyes. This was the dangerous, crafty and ruthless man she'd come to expect over the past two years. "Do you want me to rub your shoulders or not?"

Kennedy stared at him. It was obviously a trick question. Who wouldn't want the strong, maddening, sexy man touching them? But she shouldn't. Couldn't.

However, that didn't seem to matter. She twisted, scooting backward.

His hard thighs pressed against her. Heat rolled off of him…or maybe the sizzling sensation was strictly internal.

She started to pull away, but his heavy hands settled over her hips.

And she was done.

5

ASHER STARED AT the curve of Kennedy's back. The fall of her dark blond hair across her shoulders. Crap. Why had he offered to touch her?

But now that he had…

She sat there, her body stiff, almost as if she expected him to pinch her or smack her over the head with a pillow. He supposed he deserved her wariness, considering he'd worked hard over the past two years to keep her at a distance.

That wasn't going to work tonight.

Leaning forward, Asher wrapped his arm around her waist and hauled her back farther. She gasped, the sound of it shooting through him as surely as any bullet could have.

His entire body responded. The need for her throbbed at every pulse point in his body, a drum beat that reverberated through his head, urging him into action.

Settling her between his open thighs, Asher let his hands rest on the curve of her shoulders. She was stiff beneath his hold, but he wasn't sure if that was because her shoulder ached or because he had his hands on her.

"Where does it hurt?"

Kennedy leaned her head to the left, her hair sliding sideways and exposing her neck. "Right here." Her hand brushed from the base of her neck up over her shoulder.

Digging his thumb into the spot, Asher quickly found the knot in her muscle and rubbed.

She groaned but didn't pull away from his hands. He'd had enough injuries to understand why she whimpered whenever he hit a particular spot. The phrase *hurt so good* came to mind.

After a few minutes her muscles began to relax, eventually going warm and loose beneath his hands. He probably could have stopped, but he didn't. Her skin was so smooth and soft. It felt like silk against his fingers. And he couldn't quite resist the way her body melted. Her spine curved a bit. Her hips settled farther back against him.

As the quiet minutes ticked by, the space between them dwindled. He liked the way Kennedy was letting him take her weight, her lithe little body gradually collapsing against his chest. He knew relying on someone else wasn't normal for her.

She was strong and smart. Wore her efficiency like a medal around her neck and reveled in her competence and independence. He could just imagine her as a little girl, chasing after her big brother and insisting she could do anything he and his friends were doing, despite being seven years younger than the rest of them.

There were times when it was easy to forget that he was nine years older than she was. But moments like this made that difference glaring…because it was just one more reason he shouldn't want her.

Her life was just beginning, while he'd already seen the world, and been disappointed by most of it.

His hands swept down her back, moving far from their initial purpose. Over her hips. Up her arms. His fingertips skimmed her throat and across her collarbones.

He couldn't help himself. Especially when Kennedy arched into his caress, her breath catching in a throaty little sound that made his pulse thrum and his cock go rock hard.

There was no mistaking his response to her. Not with her rear settled right against the obvious ridge.

She squirmed, the curve of her ass torturing him in new and delightful ways.

"What are you doing?" he asked, his voice gruff.

Twisting her head, she stared up at him out of those delicious whiskey eyes. Heat rolled through him, matching the blaze of honeyed need he recognized in hers.

Kennedy shook her head, a denial that was probably too late for either of them to heed. Asher placed his hands on her hips, ready to push her away and do the right thing. He was playing with fire here. This wasn't going to end well for either of them.

But before he could follow through, she moved up, threaded her fingers into his hair and dragged his head down to hers. Her mouth sealed to his, hard and insistent. Unyielding. Fighting for control of the moment.

If any other woman had kissed him that way he probably would have walked away. He liked being in control, needed it to feel comfortable and in charge of the situation. There was nothing comfortable about what he felt for Kennedy. Nothing easy.

This was all kinds of messed up. Jackson was going

to kill him if he ever found out. But Asher couldn't seem to muster up the will to care. Not right now anyway.

He'd fantasized about Kennedy's mouth for a long time—deep kisses, teasing and soft licks of her tongue, those dark pink lips stretched around his hard…

A groan rolled up from deep inside his chest. *Shit*, he thought, right before giving in.

Bracketing her face with his palms, he pulled her closer. He needed a deeper taste. If he was doing this, he was damn well doing it right.

Angling her head, he licked at her lips, enjoying the way she opened for him, eager for whatever came next.

"Goddammit," he whispered right before diving inside the moist heat of her mouth.

The moment swirled around them. The scent of her enveloped him. She tasted sweet and forbidden. Like the most decadent dessert. The kind of thing you were only supposed to indulge in once in a while but always craved.

Kennedy wasn't the kind of woman to sit idly and let a man take over. Even as he maneuvered her head, she was shifting her body. Crawling into his lap without losing their connection. Taking just as much as giving.

Her tongue tangled with his, matching him stroke for stroke. Her hands wandered over his shoulders, flipping the buttons on his shirt until she could find bare skin.

A hungry little sound rolled through her throat.

Asher drank it up, keeping it all for himself.

Spreading her thighs, she settled her hips right over him, grinding down on his already throbbing erection.

Her hands raced across his skin, touching, teasing, driving him insane. With a gentle yank, she shoved his shirt down his arms to pool on the bed beside them.

Everything was a red haze, clouding out reality and any scrap of decency he'd been trying to cling to. His only thought was to finally have what he wanted. Her.

His fingers slipped beneath the hem of her shirt, pulling it off over her head and throwing it across the room, uncaring where it might land.

Pulling back, Asher let his gaze roam down her exposed body. Her bra was beige, but there was nothing plain about the way it cupped her breasts, pushing them high enough to make his mouth water. He could see the tight pink centers begging for attention through the thin fabric.

Leaning down, he sucked one deep into his mouth, relishing the soft cry of pleasure that fell from her parted lips.

Her fingers tightened where she gripped his shoulders. Her hips bucked as he lightly scraped his teeth across the distended nipple.

He could feel the heat of her as she rocked against him, searching for a relief he needed just as much. Reaching between them, he found the wet heat of her desire soaking through the thin barrier of her shorts, driving him mad.

He rubbed. She gasped, energy crackling between them.

God, he needed more of her.

His hands played across her back, stroking her soft skin. She was so warm.

His fingers pulled at the clasp of her bra, intent on freeing her so he could taste more.

But before he could undo the little hooks, her hands slammed down over his arms, pinning them to her sides. "Stop," she said, panting.

Immediately, Asher stilled. He was a lot of things, and not all of them good, but one thing he'd never do was push a woman past the point she was comfortable.

Kennedy shifted back on his lap, rolling against his pounding erection and pulling out a ragged groan.

Asher shut his eyes, searching for his good intentions. And waited for her to climb off him, but she didn't.

Her fingers stayed wrapped around his biceps. His pinky brushed against the soft skin at her waist. Her moist breath puffed against his throat.

Was she torturing him on purpose?

"Seriously, Kennedy. I only have so much willpower. You need to get up."

When she still didn't move after several seconds, Asher opened his eyes only to find her staring at him. Her gaze was enigmatic and way too thoughtful. How did she have brain cells still functioning? He felt as if his were ready to explode right along with the rest of his body.

"That wasn't what I meant," she said.

What the hell was she talking about? "I'm pretty sure there's only one meaning for *stop*. Especially when a man has his tongue and hands all over a half-naked woman."

Her lips twisted into that smart-ass grin that drove him completely nuts.

"You know what? Every time I see that chivalrous streak you seem to prefer to hide, I'm always surprised. But I shouldn't be by now."

"I don't take advantage of women. I don't have to."

Something dark twisted through her gaze. "Of course not. Not when they throw themselves at you."

"That has nothing to do with it."

"Sure it does."

Asher wrapped his hands around her hips and lifted Kennedy off his lap, depositing her onto the bed beside him. He moved to leave, but she grasped his arm.

"Seriously, Asher. I told you to stop because the camera is still rolling."

He glanced over to the corner of the room where the lens silently watched them. Immersed in Kennedy, he'd completely forgotten it was there, recording every passionate kiss, erotic sigh and demanding touch.

Thank God she hadn't, because the last thing he wanted was for some cameraman to get an eye full of naked Kennedy.

Suddenly, an overprotective and possessive wave swept through him, heating his skin and tightening every muscle in his body.

"No, that wouldn't be good."

The smirk on her face went a little more dangerous. She considered him, tilting her head to the side. "I'll erase the footage before giving the camera back to Neil."

"Who the hell is Neil? And you damn well better. Haven't you had enough brushes with public indecency?"

She flinched at his words. Asher immediately regretted them, but there was no way to take them back.

"I'm sorry," he forced out between stiff lips. Just minutes ago they'd been warm and wet beneath Kennedy's mouth. He wanted that back, even if, now that he was out from under the haze of lust, his sanity was returning.

Bounding up from the bed, Kennedy shot him a tight

look, scooped her shirt from the floor and pulled it back over her head. Then she moved to the camera, hitting a button.

Turning to face him, she crossed her arms beneath her breasts, tilted her head to the side and studied him in a way that left him feeling exposed and edgy.

"I think maybe we've figured out the key to suppressing your stutter."

"Oh, yeah, what's that?"

She walked slowly toward him. Her hips swayed, drawing his gaze. The woman was brilliantly sexy. Too sexy for her own good.

Asher licked his lips. The decadent taste of her still clung there, flooding his mouth. He wanted to kiss her again, over and over.

"Sex."

Asher blinked. "Excuse me?"

"You haven't stuttered once since this—" she wagged a finger between them "—started."

He stared at her, realizing that she was right. When he'd first started talking, his throat had been tight, his chest aching with the certainty that he wouldn't be able to do this. And he'd stuttered, not much, but a little.

Then she'd started talking back, sharing tiny pieces of herself with him, and he'd put his hands on her. From that moment on, getting more of her had been all he could think about. Obviously not the camera recording in the corner.

And he hadn't stuttered once.

BLOODY HELL.

Asher rubbed his hands up and down his face, trying to wipe away the past several hours.

He'd walked out of Kennedy's room, his body revving like a stock-car engine, high-octane need at two hundred miles per hour. His mind was spinning nearly as quickly.

It wasn't as if this would be his first sleepless night. It wasn't even his first sleepless night over a woman. But it was the first in a hell of a long time. Damn her for changing everything with a few kisses and tantalizing words.

When she'd despised him, it had been easier to suppress his desire for her. But now that he'd seen how her body responded to him...

Across the room, his cell phone buzzed, vibrating against the top of the dresser.

It was after midnight. There were only a handful of people who'd call him this late.

Crossing the room, Asher snatched up the phone and nearly groaned when he read the display screen.

Jackson Duchane was the last person he needed to talk to right now. Guilt and dread twisted his gut. Had he found out what had happened?

There was no way, not when Asher had just left Kennedy's room not twenty minutes ago. But that was immediately where his head went. How bad things would go if Jackson found out he'd touched his little sister.

A bitter taste flooded his mouth. Jackson, Knox and the team they'd built at Trident were all he had. They were his family. Had been from the moment they'd all been assigned to the same team.

But there was no question in his mind, should Jackson be forced to choose between him and Kennedy, his sister would win. As she should.

Just one more reason he needed to keep his hands off Kennedy.

"Reynolds," he said, pressing the cell to his ear.

"Hey, man. Sorry to call so late, but it's been a crazy couple days here. I have a few minutes before we get started today, so I wanted to touch base."

Asher did a quick calculation in his head, realizing that it was actually early morning where his friend was, about seven hours ahead of their location in the Caribbean.

"It's fine. I was still awake."

"I figured you might be. How'd the first day go? I know you weren't enthusiastic about taking on this project. Thanks, man, for doing it anyway."

Shit, the guilt nearly choked him.

"It went fine." Even Asher could hear the lie in his own words. Maybe his friend wouldn't notice.

The pause at the other end of the line suggested that was some serious wishful thinking.

"You sure?" Jackson finally asked.

Asher sighed, the sound of it echoing down the line and reverberating back to him. "Nothing I can't handle."

"Kennedy giving you shit?"

He really didn't want to talk about Kennedy with her older brother right now. "No more than usual. You know how we are."

Jackson made a sound, a harsh, strangled laugh. "Maybe being forced to work together will be good for both of you. I just don't understand the animosity between you."

If he knew what had happened tonight, Jackson wouldn't think his little sister being with Asher on the

Amphitrite for the next two weeks was a good idea. But it was a little late for that.

"One of these days you're going to have to explain it to me, man."

"I already have." Or he'd tried, without revealing Kennedy's secret, his insistent attraction to the man's sister or the way his body reacted whenever she was close. He had this aversion to getting his ass kicked and avoided it whenever possible.

"Not to my satisfaction."

"Tough shit."

Jackson grunted but, thank the good lord, changed the subject. "How's the production crew?"

"They tried to dress me in a three-piece suit...with a bow tie."

The loud burst of laughter made some of the heaviness in Asher's chest disappear. Part of him wanted to reach through the phone and smack Jackson in the back of the head, which was exactly what he would have done if they'd been in the same room. The rest of him simply smiled at the sound of his friend's laughter.

That's what friends were for, after all. Jackson had his back, one hundred and ten percent of the time. The man had saved his life on more than one occasion, and Asher had taken a bullet for him. The battlefield bonded you in ways everyday life just couldn't.

Besides, he could give as good as he got and had laughed his ass off plenty at Jackson's expense when his friend had first gotten together with Loralei.

"Thanks," he said, sarcasm leaking through the single word. "Your sympathy is overwhelming."

"I'm sorry. I just...the visual is too much."

"Then you'd have loved the chick who kept popping up out of nowhere to brush powder across my face."

"Makeup? They have you wearing makeup?"

Asher grunted, trying to block out the memories. Who would have thought brushes and tiny pots of colored powder could masquerade as torture devices?

"Please, tell me there are pictures of that."

He damn well hoped not. That was the last thing he needed. His man card was already in jeopardy as it was.

"Not a snowball's chance in hell."

A smile tugged at his lips. This was exactly what he'd needed, a conversation with his friend to set him back on even ground.

And remind him why touching Kennedy was a bad, bad idea. There was too much at stake and not even an amazing night with her was worth losing everything that mattered to him. And he wasn't naive enough to think starting something with her could end any other way…no woman in his life ever stuck.

Asher heard a soft, feminine voice in the background on Jackson's end. "Tell Loralei I said hi, and to give you shit."

"I'll tell her the first part. She's got the second handled just fine without your prompting. Listen, man, I have to go. Things are moving quickly here."

That was good news. Locating the *Chimera* had gained Trident some exposure, but this new find could cement their position within the salvage industry.

After this documentary aired, their visibility would increase even more. The ultimate goal was to be able to focus full-time on treasure and historical salvages and let the commercial diving side of their business, which was the only thing keeping them afloat right now, gradually fade away.

Which meant, somehow, someway, he needed to get through this documentary. This was his opportunity to contribute.

"Thanks, man. Seriously. I know doing this documentary isn't your idea of a good time. I appreciate you taking one for the team."

His resolve cemented as Jackson hung up.

Asher flopped onto the bed, arms and legs spread wide.

At least Kennedy's little stunt tonight proved one thing. He'd conquered his fear of the camera once before. He could do it again.

He simply had to find a method that didn't require him to touch Kennedy, kiss her or strip the clothes from her luscious body.

6

KENNEDY STARED AT the video playing across her computer screen. It was late. Or early. She'd meant to download the file from the camera and then go to bed. Tomorrow was going to be an interesting day. But somewhere along the way, her good intentions had flown out the window.

The first time she'd hit Play, she'd told herself it was so she could see if she could learn anything helpful from the recording.

The second time she'd just wanted to double-check before deleting it permanently.

By the fourth time she'd stopped lying to herself.

Watching Asher on the small screen of her computer got her hot. He was gorgeous, but there was more.

Things she hadn't picked up on when they were in that room together. Like the intensity pinching his face when he'd been rubbing her shoulders. The tension that had invaded his body, inch by inch, while she'd closed her eyes in bliss as he'd worked the painful knot from her muscles.

The memory of his mouth on hers, demanding and masterful. The slide of his wide hands across her back.

The more she'd watched the video, the more her body had burned. And the harder her brain had worked to convince herself this was okay.

She'd kept her distance for a long time because she didn't think Asher liked her. The evidence on that video proved he might not appreciate her as an employee, but he wanted her as a woman. And right now, she was okay with that.

She could enjoy Asher, just as she'd seen him enjoy countless women since coming to Jacksonville, and not feel one iota of remorse.

And if it helped him deal with his stutter, gave him something else to think about when the cameras were rolling, so much the better. She needed the documentary finished without any delays if she planned to make it to Seattle. Asher's issues could present a serious problem. Two birds, one stone and all that.

After sleeping for a couple of hours, Kennedy woke with more energy than she should have. It hadn't taken her long to track down Daniel in the mess. He was still a bit bleary around the edges, cradling a steaming mug of coffee in his hands.

"How do you handle living on such a small ship?" he groused, the skin around his eyes pinched tight.

Actually, the *Amphitrite* was a fairly large ship for her class and purpose. But she wasn't a cruise ship, which Kennedy would bet money was the kind of ocean experience Daniel was used to. They had stabilizers, but the ship still responded to the pitch and roll of waves.

"One of the guys doubles as our medic on board. If

you need something for seasickness, ask Tyson. He's got a bag of tricks."

Daniel shook his head. "That's not the problem. I fell out of bed. Twice."

Kennedy had to smother her laughter. Most of the crew were sharing berths, which meant beds that were no doubt much smaller than what they had at home. She and Asher were two of the few who had scored individual cabins. For a minute, Kennedy felt guilty...until she remembered how handy hers had been last night.

"Sorry. Hey, I need to talk to you about the schedule."

"What now?" Daniel's gaze narrowed as he peered up at her. Pressing her advantage, Kennedy rested her hip against the edge of the table close to him and gave him a reassuring smile.

"Just, we're still scheduled to film some underwater sequences with the dive team today, right?"

Daniel's gaze narrowed even more. "I'd thought about rearranging."

Kennedy's stomach dropped. No, that's not what she needed. Being underwater would give Asher a chance to get used to having cameras in his face without having to speak.

"Look, Asher needs a day to get accustomed to being on camera. I've seen some test footage. I promise, he's exactly what you want for this documentary. You saw him last night. He's the perfect combination of power, presence and irreverence. He's exactly the kind of man women fantasize about. I wouldn't be surprised to hear that several of the major news networks wanted to air this documentary as a prime-time special."

Kennedy dropped her voice down to a conspiratorial whisper and leaned closer. "You know, the story of the *Chimera* has become a real-life action adventure. With Asher headlining, I promise you'll be able to sell it to anyone and everyone."

"Fine," Daniel groused. "We'll get some underwater footage today, but I want him in the shots."

Kennedy suppressed a smile. That's what she'd been counting on. "I think that can be arranged."

This was the part of business she loved. The maneuvering and positioning. The back and forth, crossed swords and mental chess games that were always involved. It made her blood whoosh faster, the high of victory as addictive as any drug.

"But no more delays."

"Of course not."

Giving the man a beautiful smile, Kennedy leaned forward and patted him on the arm, as if they were best friends and had been for years.

She turned to leave, only to stop short. Asher stood several feet away, arms crossed over his chest and eyes drilling straight into her.

HE REGISTERED THE moment Kennedy realized he was there and listening to her conversation with Daniel.

Her steps faltered, but that was the only indication that his presence affected her. The rest of her expression never wavered, which meant he was gifted with the brilliance of a megawatt smile.

The thing was, he knew it wasn't real, even if it was radiantly blinding.

She was good. Her willingness to be manipulative when it suited her should have left him irritated and troubled. Instead, he was just awed at her audacity and confidence.

Rare enough qualities to find in anyone, but especially in a woman her age. It was easy to forget that she was only twenty-four.

Her minute falter didn't last long before her monstrous self-confidence was back in place and had her closing the gap between them. He expected her to stop in front of him, so she was almost beside him before he realized she intended to sail right past.

Reaching out, Asher wrapped a hand around her upper arm, pulling her to a stop. Her shoulder brushed against him, and lightning crackled across his skin.

Twisting her head, she glanced up from beneath her lashes. Was that the faint stain of a blush on her cheeks? Nope, couldn't be. Not his Kennedy.

"Where do you think you're going, cupcake?"

Her eyes flashed. Her earlier threat to smash one in his face ran through Asher's head, and he couldn't suppress the grin of challenge that touched his lips.

Laying her hand over his, Kennedy twisted her body in his direction, crowding into his personal space again.

It was a move she used often, and one that probably worked well for her. He could see how her bold self-assurance would set most men firmly outside their comfort zone.

The problem was, that was exactly where he wanted her, even if he shouldn't…as close as he could get her.

She ripped her arm from his grasp. "I was just coming to find you." Pushing up on her toes, she gripped his shirt in her hands and tugged until he bent, bringing her mouth to his ear and whispering, "I've bought us a day. We need you ready to go by tomorrow."

Wrapping his hand around the nape of her neck, Asher tried to ignore the silky feel of her hair as it threaded through his fingers. He tilted her head and brought his own mouth to the delicate shell of her ear.

He wanted to lick it, to tug the round curve of her lobe between his teeth and watch the way she'd squirm as he sucked.

"Cupcake, I'm always ready."

Asher relished the way Kennedy's skin flushed and her pupils dilated. Her mouth parted, those luscious lips glistening temptingly.

There was a masochistic part of him that delighted in knowing she reacted to him, even if he couldn't let himself do anything about it.

Taking a step backward, he tried to clear the scent of her from his lungs.

"So I hear we're going down with the dive team."

"*You* are."

"Oh, no, princess. If I'm going down there today, so are you."

Almost before the words were out of his mouth she was shaking her head. "I'm not a diver."

"Bullshit. If Jackson wouldn't let you go without shooting lessons, I know good and well that he took you diving."

"Yes, I've been, but that doesn't make me a diver. There'll be enough people down there, I don't want to get in the way."

The thing was, Asher wanted her with him. He'd seen pictures of the *Chimera*. Had watched hours of footage when they were evaluating the stability of the wreckage. But he'd never seen the ship in person.

And for some reason, he wanted to share the thrill with Kennedy. "Do you want me to dive today?"

Her answer was quick and clipped. "Yes."

"Then you're coming with me."

KENNEDY HUNG BACK, watching as the team prepped to descend for their first dive of the day. The excavation team gathered the equipment they'd need and splashed off the platform and into the water.

Three cameramen followed, carrying cameras specially designed to capture images underwater.

Asher walked up beside her. It wasn't the first time she'd seen him in a wet suit, but that didn't stop her pulse from speeding up at the sight. The neoprene clung to his body, outlining every thick muscle and bulge.

Her mouth went dry and her stomach fluttered.

"Quit stalling, cupcake. In you go."

She half expected him to shove her straight off the diving platform and braced her body for the impact. Asher chuckled, the low rumble skittering across her skin in a way that made her body hum.

Hell, at this point it would be worth getting wet just to extinguish the burning need flaming through her.

She had to get a grip. There was nothing wrong with wanting the man, or even with acting on that desire. But she needed to stay in complete control of herself and the situation.

It was bad enough that she was drawn to Asher in such a physical, all encompassing way. Already, he was difficult to stay away from. If she gave in…that would be so much more difficult.

And she couldn't afford to develop any more ties that might make leaving Jacksonville more difficult.

Checking her equipment one last time, Kennedy slipped off the platform and into the water.

It was warm and welcoming, but she'd never get used to those first few seconds of panicked breathing as water covered her head. It was mind over instinct, her lungs heaving with alarm even as she tried to take steady, even breaths.

The muted sound of a splash echoed around her. Asher's tight body rocketed past her before stopping to glide back in her direction.

A sense of calm settled over her as she watched him, powerful and graceful in the water. Much like her brother, Asher was in his element here, which shouldn't have surprised her but somehow did.

She'd never really thought about Asher in that way. Why he was drawn to the water. Why he'd become a SEAL. She'd always known Jackson had followed his love of diving, but had Asher?

Turning, he began to tread water only a foot or so away. Sunlight streamed through the surface above them, sparkling off his mask and making his eyes appear even darker, more intense.

A shiver raced down Kennedy's spine.

Using hand signals, Asher asked if she was okay, and when she gave him an affirmative, indicated they should start the descent to the wreck.

A tiny flutter of panic erupted in her chest. Something on her face must have given her away because Asher grasped her upper arms and pulled her close. She could see the question in his eyes through the thin plastic masks covering their faces.

Shaking her head, Kennedy tried to tell him she was fine, although that wasn't quite true.

She'd been diving before. Not only was her brother a master diver, but her dad and mom were both amateurs. Everyone else in her family loved to be under the water, which she'd never understood.

She didn't like the sensation of pressure on her chest that came with descending deep beneath the waves. Whenever she was under, she had to constantly fight the panic that something was going to go wrong and she was going to drown.

But she did it anyway. She tried to push out of Asher's hold. His fingers tightened, keeping her in place.

One hand dragged up her arm, tangled into her hair and tipped her head back so he could get a better look at her. Those intense green eyes speared her straight through.

Kennedy wanted to blink, look away, something, but she couldn't. Not for the first time around this man, she felt bare and vulnerable from nothing more than his gaze. Asher might be brash, bold and overly confident, but he was also observant. Too observant for her peace of mind.

Kicking out with his powerful legs, Asher sent them both to the surface only a few feet overhead. They broke free, and the pressure squeezing Kennedy's chest eased, as it always did.

Asher spit the regulator out of his mouth, letting it splash down into the water beside him, and pushed the mask onto the top of his head. Kennedy did the same, but he didn't let her go. His fingers stayed entwined in her wet hair.

"Why didn't I know that you're afraid of diving?"

"Because I'm not."

He frowned, his eyes narrowing. "Don't lie to me,

Kennedy. I'm intimately familiar with the signs of fear and could see it all over your face."

"I'm not afraid of diving." Because she refused to be. "It's not my favorite thing in the world, but I've got plenty of hours under my belt. Not as many as you, Jackson or Knox, but enough. I know what I'm doing."

The grooves between his eyes deepened. "Why would you spend so much time doing something you don't enjoy?"

"Because the rest of my family does it? Because I work for a diving company? Because I don't like giving in to anything, including fear?"

It took Kennedy a few seconds to realize just how much her response revealed. Way more than she'd intended.

Asher's face relaxed. His hold on her gentled, not that it had been particularly harsh. But now, instead of feeling like solid bands against her skin, his fingers stroked, soothed.

Threatened to suck her into something she shouldn't want.

"You know what? I changed my mind, you don't have to dive with me."

A couple of weeks ago, his statement would have pissed her off. She would have seen it as a backhanded challenge. A dig at something she wasn't good at. Today, she didn't see any of the underlying antagonism that had swirled between them.

Right now, Asher watched her with understanding and acceptance in his eyes.

Which only made her resolve that much stronger. "Yes, I do."

"Why? The team is fine. The camera crew are experienced and know what they're doing."

"I'm fine, Asher. And I'm going down there. Now, will you please let me go, so I can do my job?"

A smile bloomed across his face. Before she realized what he'd intended to do, his mouth settled over hers. Salty and hot. Tempting and reassuring. His tongue breeched her lips, sweeping inside and sending a blast of red-hot need coursing through her veins.

How could the man turn her inside out with nothing more than his mouth?

The kiss was quick and vivid, passionate. Over when it had barely begun.

Picking up her regulator where it floated on the surface of the water, he cleared it, said, "Cupcake, you have more balls than most of the men I know," and stuck it into her open mouth before she could even respond.

It wasn't until he let her go that Kennedy realized just how dangerous that kiss had been. Out in the open, anyone from the Trident team could have seen them. And that would not have been good.

What the hell had Asher been thinking?

Anxiety mixed with residual desire, twisting in her belly and completely eclipsing any fear that remained.

Gently, Asher pulled the mask from the top of her head and fit it back over her face. He replaced his own mask, but it didn't hide the cocky grin twisting his lips. *Bastard*, she thought, though there was no heat behind the word.

Twining his fingers with hers, he led her back down into the water. And didn't let her go. The constant pressure of his hand in hers helped to steady her nerves.

They took their time, descending slowly into the

murky depths. And suddenly, she was there, right in front of them—the *Chimera*.

If they'd been above, Kennedy would have lost her breath. The ship was that gorgeous and tragic.

She'd seen plenty of pictures over the past several months. Even some video footage from the remote-controlled cameras they'd sent down to survey. But it wasn't the same.

And abruptly, Kennedy understood why Jackson had risked so much to find the wreck. She hadn't before, never quite getting her brother's obsession with this ship.

People swam around the broken pieces of the ship, cataloguing, painstakingly preserving and recovering. But not even the flurry of activity could displace the eerie quality to the wreckage.

One hundred and fifty years ago she was a hundred feet above, floating on the water just like the *Amphitrite*. But one powerful storm had sent her tumbling straight to the bottom of the sea, ripping a jagged hole into the side of her wooden hull.

Kennedy felt a squeeze on her fingers and looked down to where Asher's hand cupped hers. Her gaze traveled up to his face, where she saw the same expression of awe and wonder that she knew must be filling hers.

7

ASHER FLOATED, SOAKING in his first encounter with the *Chimera*. He wasn't as into the historical side of things as Jackson and Knox were. He enjoyed diving, loved the men he called brothers and had been more than happy to open Trident and start a business together. If they'd told him they wanted to learn underwater ballet, he probably would have been on board.

Okay, maybe not…

But his desire to be part of this had less to do with actually discovering the wreck than it did with continuing to be part of the family he'd found with Jackson and Knox. He'd been pleased for his friend when Jackson's years of work had paid off and he'd found the ship. And happy from a business standpoint when Knox's efforts had secured their exclusive salvage rights.

He wanted the business to succeed, and in order to do that they needed the funds from the salvage. Were desperate to recover the gold everyone prayed was hidden inside the wreck.

But floating there, Kennedy's small hand gripped firmly in his, he stared at the majesty of the *Chimera* and couldn't stop the wave of emotion that stampeded through him.

She was gorgeous in a tragic way. For some reason, she reminded him of the empty house he'd come home to after Krista left him. Desolate and vacant, absent of the sounds, smells and sights that should have inhabited her.

Against the backdrop of the gorgeous turquoise Caribbean Sea, red, yellow, purple and orange fish swam in and out of the wreck, their liveliness somehow punctuating the tragedy of what had happened here so long ago.

Asher couldn't even imagine the panic the crew must have felt in the middle of the storm that had brought her down. Had they reached a point of resignation, knowing they would never see their loved ones again?

Had his father experienced that same moment? Thought of the wife and son he'd left behind?

A lump crowded his throat. Squeezing his eyes tight, Asher forced the thoughts away. This wasn't the time or place for his own grief.

Kennedy's fingers squeezed his harder. He didn't look over at her. Didn't want her to see the evidence of yet another weakness he couldn't seem to conquer.

Luckily, at that moment two of the cameramen swam up to them.

Kennedy disentangled their fingers. Asher tried to keep hold of her but couldn't. He didn't like the idea of her letting him go, although he refused to examine the feeling too closely.

Before descending, Daniel had given him some instructions for the shots he needed today. The cameras would follow him as he inspected the wreckage and the work their salvage crew was conducting inside.

For the next hour, Asher tried to ignore the cameras, pretending they weren't present. He watched one of the dive team document the position of an artifact from one of the crew cabins before stowing it so he could take it up. There was no telling what the barnacle-encrusted hunk of metal was. He'd hand it off to the preservation crew, who would stabilize the piece for transportation to their lab where the painstaking process of uncovering years of grime and salt would begin.

Through it all, Asher was aware of Kennedy's every movement. Most of the time, she stuck close to him, at least close enough that he could find her out of the corner of his vision. After seeing the fear in her eyes earlier, he'd been uneasy about letting her get too far away.

Consulting his dive computer, Asher realized it was about time to ascend and was ready to make a gesture to round up the crew and head that way, when a commotion off to his left caught his attention.

Then Kennedy rocketed through his line of sight.

Turning, Asher took in a cluster of people, Kennedy and two of the cameramen. For the first time he realized one of the cameras was free, sinking toward the sea floor several meters below.

One of the cameramen—Asher thought his name was Neil—had the other, John, limp and lifeless, grasped in his arms.

Oh shit.

Kennedy looked around, frantic, and when her gaze collided with his, he could see sheer panic suffusing her face.

Using every ounce of strength he had, Asher kicked

out straight for them. In a few seconds flat he assessed
the situation. John was unconscious, but his mouth was
still sealed around the regulator, holding it in place.
Still, this wasn't good. At all.

Forcing himself in between the cluster of people, he
pressed his fingers to John's jugular, relieved to feel a
pulse, even if it was faint. The bubbles drifting from
the regulator told him the man was at least breathing,
even if the puffs were shallow and erratic.

He had no idea what was going on, and he couldn't
really evaluate him down here. They needed to get him
out of the water and couldn't afford to waste any time.

Wrapping an arm across the cameraman's chest,
Asher kicked up, dragging the dead weight with him.
There was a fine line between getting the patient to
the deck and potential medical help as quickly as possible and rising so quickly that he risked adding complications to whatever had gone wrong. Asher pushed
that line as much as he could, ascending faster than he
probably should have.

His own body protested, pain lancing through his
ears and teeth, his vision graying out. But he pushed
on, ignoring the small signs because getting help was
more important.

It felt like forever before they finally broke through
the surface. Adrenaline and dread pulsed through Asher
with each labored breath. Yelling up to the team on the
deck, he had them scrambling to get the cameraman
back on to the ship.

His battlefield training kicked in. Peeling equipment
from the man, he tried to assess the situation. Luckily,
Tyson hadn't been part of the crew diving today and
someone must have alerted him to the problem.

Skidding on to the deck beside him, Tyson asked, "What happened?"

"I'm not sure." Thankfully, John was breathing on his own, but his pulse was thready and weak.

From behind him, Kennedy's voice sounded. Her hand settled on his shoulder, soothing him in a way he hadn't realized he'd needed. "He collapsed, going unconscious. Luckily, Neil was paying attention, and Asher got him up here as soon as possible."

Tyson gave John a quick assessment. "Without proper equipment I can't say for sure, but he definitely needs medical attention. Fast. It's possible he's having a heart attack, or descended too quickly and developed an embolism."

Shooting to his feet, Asher headed into the wheelhouse. Picking up the mic, he sent out a rescue request over the radio. Within a few seconds, they had a response from an OPBAT team, a joint task force between the US Coast Guard, DEA and the Bahamian Government. They normally concentrated on drug smuggling, but thanks to Knox and Avery's experience with them several months ago, they were aware of the *Amphitrite's* location and purpose out here.

Returning to the deck, Asher couldn't stop the nervous energy flowing through him. There wasn't really an outlet for it. Tyson was doing his job, stabilizing the guy as much as possible.

John was in his late fifties, but Asher had been assured those diving on the production crew had logged hundreds of scuba hours and could handle the unique requirements of this assignment. That didn't necessarily rule out the possibility of an embolism, but it made a heart attack more likely.

Ten minutes after he'd placed the distress call, the familiar *thwap, thwap, thwap* of a helicopter could be heard in the distance. He'd ridden plenty of helos in his career, into and out of nightmarish situations.

His body reacted with a familiar response, adrenaline rushing into his bloodstream. The helicopter pilot communicated with the captain, but Asher didn't need the instructions being sent down. He knew how to handle a helo rescue, especially on water.

Clearing everyone away from the injured man, he watched as the Coast Guard team lowered their basket. Once it was guided down to the deck, Asher, Tyson and Neil secured the unconscious man in the basket.

Asher held the line to keep it steady, as a winch in the helicopter slowly raised it back again.

Ten minutes after they'd arrived, the helicopter was turning and disappearing into the distance.

He should have felt better.

He didn't.

Energy buzzed through his blood. It bothered him to watch the man disappear into the bright blue sky without knowing how he would fare.

On the other side of the deck, Daniel and Neil, who was still dripping wet from the dive, stood with their heads together.

Kennedy was close by, speaking to several of the crew before finally turning in his direction. Even across the deck, he could feel the impact of her gaze as it landed on him. The heat, the understanding, the expectation and concern.

More than anything right now, he needed Kennedy's cool, calm demeanor. Her reassurance that everything would be fine and the man he'd just rescued wouldn't die. He'd seen enough death to last his entire lifetime. Knew, intimately, the impact of receiving that visit from someone in uniform informing you that your loved one was dead.

He'd never forget the keening, inhuman sound his mother had made, collapsing to her knees in the middle of their open doorway.

But it was that pervading need, a weakness that left him so vulnerable, which kept his feet rooted to the spot.

He didn't want to need Kennedy. Couldn't let himself go there, not with anyone, but especially not with her.

The familiar tension seized his muscles, tightening his throat and pressing hard against his lungs, when she walked across the deck toward him.

He wanted to snipe at her, make some smart-ass comment that would make her reverse direction and leave him alone. But the words wouldn't come.

Stopping in front of him, Kennedy asked, "Are you all right?"

"Fine." He forced the single word past the tightness constricting his throat. He would not give into his stutter. Not today. Not with her.

The corners of Kennedy's lips pulled into a frown, but she didn't push. Instead, she said carefully, "I just talked with Neil."

"Great."

Kennedy's eyes narrowed. "The production company is sending someone to gather John's family and bring them to Nassau. Daniel's already in contact with the hospital. We should know something about his condition soon."

"I'm glad."

Kennedy's sharp gaze raked across his face. Asher drew in tight, trying to keep a lid on the churning emotions threatening to bubble up inside him.

"Daniel's suspended production for the rest of the day."

Thank God for that, at least. It was the right thing to do with a member of his team being medevaced. Not to mention, Asher was in no shape to perform in front of a camera at the moment.

"So, I was thinking we needed to take advantage of the opportunity and get you some more experience in front of the camera. Daniel wants to work on some inside shots tomorrow, since he can film those even though he's now down one cameraman."

The thought of being alone in a room with Kennedy right now sent his head spinning. He was already fighting the need to crush her against his body, to lose himself in the relief of her hot mouth.

He should say no. Find some excuse.

But one look at the determination in Kennedy's expression was all it took to realize that wasn't an option.

This was going to end very badly.

LEADING ASHER INTO the office the film crew had occupied yesterday, she closed and locked the door behind them. Unlike last night, when the ship had been quiet and most everyone already turned in for the night, today everyone was up and about. The last thing she needed was someone interrupting.

"What are we doing?"

"Crash course in media training."

"Didn't we do that last night?"

"Not really." What they'd done was almost have sex.

"You avoided the camera, which was fine for last night, but a little difficult to do come tomorrow when Daniel will expect you to, you know, talk directly into it."

She watched Asher's jaw go hard, his teeth grinding together in an unpleasant way that made her own jaw ache.

"Why don't we start with you propped on the edge of the desk like you were before."

Turning, Asher headed for the desk, setting his hips against it and wrapping those massive hands around the edge. Today he wasn't wearing the slacks and button-down shirt, and she kind of missed them. But he was just as sexy in a pair of board shorts and a dark gray T-shirt that clung to his chest.

"All right, you've got me where you want me, cupcake. Now what?"

Oh, he was going to pay for that.

"Why don't we start by going through the questions Daniel will be asking? Get you comfortable with giving the answers on camera."

Asher nodded. His mouth was drawn tight, and his face was pinched, giving him a severe and dangerous look. But right now, what she wanted was for him to relax.

"Take a deep breath, Ash. It's just the two of us in here. No pressure."

"That's n-not entirely true, is it?" His forehead crinkled right between the slashing lines of his eyebrows. "If I can't get this right, I'm going to screw up everything for this documentary. For you and Trident. Not to mention Jackson and Knox who are depending on me to pull this off. Trust me, there's pressure."

Kennedy shook her head. It was hard not to notice

the way Asher's body tensed whenever his mouth mangled a word. It bothered her, how he seemed to brace for some backlash.

It made her want to wrap her arms around him and hold on tight...a very dangerous inclination considering Asher most likely wouldn't appreciate it. In fact, he'd probably see the gesture as some indication that she thought him weak.

Men and their fragile egos. His fear and stutter didn't make him weak. It made him human.

She liked him even more because of the imperfection.

"By the way, you were amazing with John. I don't think he'd have had a chance if you weren't there."

"That's not true. I didn't do much, just got him to the surface."

"Faster than anyone else could have. Were you even aware that it took the rest of us a good fifteen more minutes?"

His hands curled tighter around the edge of the desk. "No."

"Like I said, frogman, you saved his life."

This time, Asher simply shrugged, again trying to deflect her praise, almost as if he didn't trust it.

Slowly, Kennedy walked across the room. He watched her, his eyes tracking her every movement. Stopping in front of him, Kennedy tipped her head back and stared into him.

"You're a hero, Ash. You and I might not always get along, but that doesn't mean I don't recognize the truth."

His only answer was a deepening frown.

This close, she could feel the heat of him, seeping straight through her skin and into her bloodstream, like some potent drug. His scent filled her lungs, adding to her intoxication.

"So, let's talk about this stutter."

His face pinched tight. She could see the swirl of emotions there that he really didn't want to share—anxiety, apprehension, determination and frustration.

"What about it?"

"Have you always had it?"

His eyes flashed with a pain that was so deep and stark it nearly took her breath away, and she wasn't even the one feeling it. She almost regretted asking the question. Almost. Because something told her whatever was behind that emotion, he needed to share and someone needed to listen.

She was happy to be that someone. Especially if it helped keep her project on track.

"No. It developed after my dad died and my mother left."

Asher's words lanced straight through Kennedy's chest. They were so cool and bland. But no one experienced that kind of thing without having emotional scars left behind.

And his stutter was proof of that.

"That must have been rough."

"The stuttering? Yeah, it was difficult not to be able to communicate with the kids at school. To panic at even the thought of being called on in class. To have the words in your brain, on your tongue, and not be able to force them out is…frightening."

"I can imagine," Kennedy murmured. "But I meant losing both of your parents so suddenly."

Asher just stared at her out of those deep green eyes. If she hadn't seen the pounding pulse just beneath his jaw or the way his fingers gripped the desk so tightly that his knuckles were turning white, she might have believed the placid exterior he was trying to present.

Even a week ago she might have bought the act. But not today.

"It sounds like your grandmother really cared about you. Wanted to help you."

"She loved me unconditionally. The only person in my life I can really say that about."

A lump formed in Kennedy's throat. Nope, she wasn't going to give in to the emotion welling inside her chest. It wasn't helpful and would only serve to push Asher away…and she was probably close enough to that happening as it was.

"It's obvious you don't suffer from the stutter as much as you used to."

"No, back then it happened almost every time I opened my mouth. Now the stutter rarely surfaces, unless I'm under extreme stress."

"What changed?"

He shrugged, his stiff shoulders lifting and dropping. Last night he'd soothed her own tense muscles. Kennedy wished he'd let her return the kindness now, but knew he wouldn't.

"I grew up."

"You stopped worrying that your world was going to go spinning off its axis again?"

The corner of his mouth twisted up. "Maybe. Probably. I made the baseball team my freshman year of high school and found a group of kids I could identify with."

No doubt he'd found people who accepted him for who he was, stutter and all. The anxiety lessened so the stutter lessened.

Which was precisely what they needed to do now.

Kennedy let a smile bloom across her face. She watched an answering one twitch at the corners of his lips. It was a start. Walking backward, she didn't stop until she was standing right next to the camera again.

"So, why don't we start with some background on how Trident discovered the *Chimera*?"

Asher's gaze flickered to the camera at her right. She didn't bother telling him it wasn't turned on. She wanted him to think that it was, but she didn't actually need the footage—definitely didn't need any more to tempt her.

He took a deep breath, filling his already wide chest with air and holding it for several seconds before letting go.

"When I m-mentioned to Jackson and Knox that I was thinking about retiring, they both protested."

"Why?"

The question really had nothing to do with the point of the exercise, because she didn't imagine Daniel would really care about the answer. But she did. She'd always wondered. None of the guys talked about their time with the SEALs much. Over the years she'd tried to press Jackson for details, but had quickly learned it wasn't a subject he liked to discuss, especially when he was home.

"Why?"

"Why was it time to move on to something else? From what Jackson and Knox have said, you were an amazing soldier."

Asher made a quick, jerky, dismissive movement with his hand. It took Kennedy a few moments to realize she'd embarrassed him.

"We'd gotten close over the years, were lucky to

have worked together since Jackson and Knox joined the SEALs. But I'm a couple years older. My body was starting to feel the effects of such a physically demanding job, and it was time for me to move on to something else…before my weakness cost someone their life. The team is only as good as the weakest link, and I refused to become that link."

Something tight squeezed her chest. Kennedy could imagine Asher's struggle, pitting his love and dedication for his job, and the guys who'd become like family, against the fear that he was becoming a liability to those same men. He constantly put the needs of others above his own.

She wondered who put his needs first? And as much as she wanted to say Jackson and Knox, she wasn't entirely certain that was true. By his own admission, Asher had gone into the business his two friends wanted instead of doing whatever he'd hoped to do.

"So you started Trident because you wanted to continue diving?"

"No, we started Trident because Jackson is a hell of a salesman."

Kennedy chuckled. "Yeah, he is, isn't he?" When her brother wanted something, he went after it and wouldn't take no for an answer—from anyone.

He'd been tenacious, working tirelessly to secure clients for Trident when they'd first opened. He'd taken some shitty jobs—they all had—in order to build the business.

Luckily, fate had brought him together with Loralei's father at Lancaster Diving and Salvage. Without Loralei, Trident never would have found the *Chimera*. And Jackson never would have met his future wife.

Kennedy loved her soon-to-be sister-in-law. She and Jackson were perfect together.

"He told us the story of the *Chimera* and how the legend of it had been handed down for generations in your family." Asher gave her another shrug. "I didn't have anything better to do."

Such a ringing endorsement for a lifetime of commitment. And if she hadn't seen Asher give one hundred and ten percent to Trident over the past two years she might wonder if he was truly dedicated to their success. But she had no doubt.

Even if he hadn't been bound to the company, it was becoming obvious that Asher would have done absolutely anything for Jackson and Knox.

"I got so tired of hearing that as my bedtime story," Kennedy mused. "Jackson didn't mind the hidden treasure and high seas drama, but *I* wanted fairy-tale princesses."

Asher laughed. "You're such a girl."

Just to taunt him, Kennedy ran her hands over her breasts, hips and along the curve of her ass, tossing him a wicked grin, "And don't you forget it."

Asher shifted, his expression going sharp and a predatory glint flashing through his eyes. "Not possible," he said, his voice low and rough enough to send a shiver racing down her spine.

Well, that had backfired. Or maybe it hadn't. From the moment they'd parted last night her body had been left simmering. She'd tried to ignore the need pulsing beneath her skin.

It wasn't working.

"Do you have any idea how difficult it is to be the

only woman surrounded by all you big, dangerous, military men?"

"Honey, you have every damn one of us wrapped around your little finger and you know it."

She tried to bite back the words but didn't succeed. "You aren't."

"The hell I'm not."

Kennedy stared at him. That was the last thing she'd expected him to say.

"Then why have you spent the past two years taunting me? What did I do?"

Asher shifted, his hips rubbing restlessly against the edge of the desk. "You d-didn't d-do anything."

Kennedy heard his words. She registered the stutter, nothing new. But for some reason, she loved the little halt in his voice.

To her, Asher Reynolds had been perfect. Gorgeous, powerful, determined, sarcastic, witty, sexy as hell. Every woman's fantasy and nightmare together. He was untouchable and so utterly superb. Like the most exclusive and expensive bottle of wine she could never afford to taste.

She could feel the tension rolling off him as he waited for her reaction to his stuttered words. It wasn't the first time she'd noticed him do this. But before, she'd simply brushed it off, thinking it was better not to acknowledge the slip and add to his embarrassment.

But maybe…

"You know, I like your stutter."

"You wh-wh-what?"

"I like it. It's cute."

His entire expression went cold. "That's not funny, Kennedy. I don't appreciate you making fun of me."

"I'm not. And I mean it, although maybe cute is the wrong word because no one could ever describe you as cute. Come on, you've looked in the mirror before and you know exactly your impact on women. I'm absolutely certain every female within a ten-mile radius wants you. So you freeze in front of a camera and stutter…it makes you real."

He continued to stare at her, but Kennedy couldn't stay still. Taking several steps nearer, she closed the gap between them, until their bodies were practically flush. She tipped her head back, looking into his eyes.

"I know you see it as a weakness, and maybe it is. But, hell, Asher, it's the only one you've got. You're smart, can handle any situation put in front of you with calm and confidence. Without that tiny flaw the rest of the world would never be able to measure up or compete. It gives us mere mortals a chance."

8

HER WORDS STUNNED HIM. But he was even more shocked when Kennedy leaned in, her hands pressed tight against his chest as she sealed her mouth to his.

The kiss was pure heaven and excruciating hell all rolled into one. Because before he could even react and pull her closer, Kennedy was gone.

She backed away. Asher's hands rose, chasing after her, fisting around empty air.

Her words had scorched through him almost as surely as that kiss. She didn't think less of him because of his fear and stutter, but it was more than that. She *liked* it. Thought it made him unique.

That floored him. Especially after years of being teased and taunted because of it. It was more than he ever could have expected, especially from Kennedy.

It wasn't as if he'd provided her any reason to be sympathetic toward him, which was the best he could have hoped for.

But that was what gave her words a ring of truth. She had no reason to lie or sugarcoat anything. So when she said something to him, he could take it at face value.

Which only made his body burn hotter, especially where her hand had pressed into his chest.

"Let's get back to work."

He opened his mouth, but nothing came out. She might like his stutter, but that didn't necessarily mean it would disappear. His throat felt swollen and scratchy, too tight to let sound and words pass through. Asher's gaze moved to the unblinking black eye of the camera lens pointed straight at him.

It would pick up every hesitation, magnifying it and amplifying it.

"Hey," Kennedy's soft voice pulled his attention. She watched him, her expression carefully neutral and easy. "Just focus on me."

Slowly, her hands moved up her body, over her belly and breasts to the button at the top of her shirt. And she flicked it open.

For a second he thought maybe she was warm. The room was small, and they were in the middle of the Caribbean. His own temperature spiked when she reached for another button and pushed it through the tiny hole holding it closed.

"What are you doing?"

"Giving you something else to think about."

"This isn't a good idea, Kennedy."

"You've already said that, but I'm a big girl and I can make my own decisions."

Asher stood there, powerless to do anything but watch as she swept the soft cotton shirt off her shoulders. It fluttered to the floor at her feet.

The bra she was wearing should have been labeled a lethal weapon. Why the hell was she wearing lingerie designed to drive a man to his knees?

It was candy-apple red and more lace than actual material. He caught tantalizing glimpses of skin through the strategic holes in the fabric. The swollen points of her nipples jutted straight out, silently begging for his attention.

His cock went rock hard.

Her skin was sun-kissed golden brown. Tiny freckles ran along her shoulders and down the swell of her chest.

God, he wanted to taste her. To run his tongue over every inch of her body and lap her up.

"Stop," he somehow managed to croak out when she reached for the button holding her shorts closed. "For the love of all that's holy, stop."

Kennedy froze, her fingers wrapped in the waistband. She swallowed, her warm whiskey gaze sharp and searching as it roamed his face. "Do you really mean that?"

"Yes. No," he groaned out.

A sinful smile tugged at her lips, and something dangerous flashed across her face. This woman, this tempting siren of a woman, was going to be the death of him. And he'd deserve every second of torture that came before. But at the moment, Asher couldn't remember why this was a bad idea.

He'd watched her and wanted her for so long.

She flicked the button on her shorts open. The sound of her zipper, metal grinding against metal, was loud in his ears and the final straw.

Standing up, Asher stilled when Kennedy shook her head.

"Nope. You can't touch."

"What?" he asked, his voice incredulous. The woman

was giving him a strip tease and expected him to keep his hands to himself?

She was crazy. Or wickedly, wickedly devious.

Or both.

"You get through the rest of these questions without hesitating, and then you can have your reward."

She was offering herself like some prize at the bottom of a Cracker Jack box. Part of that pissed Asher off. Kennedy was more than something to be won.

She was the kind of woman you earned, and spent the rest of your goddamn life trying to keep up the pretense that you deserved her.

She was every man's fantasy of forever.

Which was why he shouldn't touch her. He'd tried forever and had no desire to try it again. Even his wife, a woman who'd stood up before God, their family and friends and professed to love him, had walked away without a thought.

No, their marriage hadn't been perfect. They'd fought and irritated each other. But he'd been blindsided when he'd returned home to an empty house.

Asher had thought they were happy. He'd given everything he could to Krista, and it still hadn't been enough.

It was never enough.

But the stakes were even higher with Kennedy. She wanted him now, but she'd decide he wasn't good enough, just like all the others. And this time he wouldn't just lose his home or his belongings.

He'd lose his friends, his family and the business he'd poured all his energy into.

But how was he supposed to resist with her standing in front of him in nothing but matching red lace panties and a bra?

He was human. He'd been fighting his desire for too long. He couldn't fight anymore.

"Then you better hurry with those questions, because you've got about fifteen minutes before I say to hell with it and give you exactly what you're asking for, little girl."

"I keep telling you, I'm not a little girl."

Asher let his gaze meander across Kennedy's body. Her breasts swelled over the cups of her bra, threatening to spill out with every ragged breath.

At least he wasn't the only one buzzing with need.

Her hips rounded nicely, the perfect hold for him to grasp and pull her tight against his own body. The smooth plane of her belly, the skin there a little lighter than the rest of her. Smooth, tanned legs that he could imagine wrapped around his waist.

She was playing with fire, but he was afraid that he was the one about to get burned.

"I'm well aware of that."

THIS WHOLE EXERCISE had been designed to take Asher's mind off his fears. However, it was backfiring because Kennedy couldn't remember a single one of the questions she'd prepared to ask him.

The way he was watching her, like a jungle cat playing with his prey, made her throat go dry and her tongue stick to the roof of her mouth.

Her entire body hummed with energy.

Asher Reynolds was dangerous. That was part of his appeal. His tattoos, the pale scar across his lip. The way he carried himself, always alert, always prepared, as if forever anticipating a problem and prepared to meet it head-on.

But those same things that made him appealing also made him aloof. It was becoming obvious to Kennedy that the scar on his lip wasn't the only one he carried, although it might be the only one he let anyone see.

Asher didn't like to admit weakness—she didn't know many men who did. He kept people at arm's length. Hell, as far as she knew, Jackson and Knox were the only true friends he had...the only people he'd ever let in.

And if she was looking for more from him that might be a problem, because any woman who wanted to crack his smooth outer shell was going to have her work cut out for her. So it was good this was just about sex.

"Explain the preservation process," Kennedy finally managed to croak out.

His lips twisted into a smirk, the kind that she knew meant he was playing with her and delighting in the mental games about to take place.

Oh, hell.

She enjoyed verbally sparring with him. It heated her blood just as much as the kisses they'd shared, stimulating her in a way she'd never experienced before... and liked.

She should have been cold, standing there in nothing but her panties and bra, but she wasn't. The energy humming beneath her skin had little to do with her lack of clothing and everything to do with the dangerous man staring at her out of those hooded green eyes.

"Do you really want to know about the preservation process?"

Kennedy swallowed hard. "Yes."

His lips tugged up at one corner, almost impercep-
tibly.

"What do I get if I answer correctly?"

"The knowledge that you're intelligent and can ver-
balize coherently?"

Asher shifted, crossing his arms over his chest in a
way that made his shoulders and biceps bulge against
the soft fabric of his T-shirt. *God help her.*

"That's not what I want."

Kennedy licked her lips, slowly, seductively. Her
heart thumped frantically behind the wall of her chest.

"What do you want?"

His gaze flashed and then narrowed. She'd seen that
expression before. Asher was shrewd. And he thought
he had her backed into a corner.

Surging up from the edge of the desk, he closed
the space between them in two quick strides. Self-
preservation kicked in, maybe a little late, and had
Kennedy taking an instinctive step backward.

But she didn't get far.

Cupping the nape of her neck, Asher stopped her
momentum. His hold wasn't hard, and she could have
broken it, but she didn't. The moment he touched her,
everything inside her just…stopped. And waited.

Angling her head back so she was looking up at him,
he said, "What I want is you on your knees."

She sucked in a gasp, not because she was startled
by his admission, but because the moment he'd said the
words in that low, smooth voice of his, she'd wanted
the same thing.

But she'd been sparring with this man long enough
to keep her response locked down tight.

"We don't always get what we want."

His fingers tangled in her hair, taking a strand and stroking it. "Cupcake, you know me better than that."

Tingles erupted across her scalp. She couldn't stop the shiver that raced down her spine. And, damn the man, the tilt of his smile said he saw everything.

Why the hell was she fighting so hard on this? Merely because that's what she'd been doing for the past two years? Or because she enjoyed the spice that layer of tension added to the energy arcing between them?

Shrugging her shoulders, Kennedy tossed him a little half grin and said, "Okay," before starting to sink down to the floor.

She didn't get far. His hand at the nape of her neck prevented her from following through.

"I didn't think you'd actually do it."

She lifted a single eyebrow. "Really? Now who doesn't know whom? We've been facing off for two years, Asher, and you didn't think I'd take your challenge seriously?"

He laughed, the sound rich and warm as it melted over her.

"Well, I'll be dammed."

"Besides, you assumed I'd see being on my knees as some kind of fine to be paid." Kennedy licked her lips. She didn't mean to, but it just…happened. "I see it as more of a reward…for me."

Asher groaned. His hand in her hair tightened and his mouth closed in on hers. Strong, sure and deadly to her equilibrium.

There was nothing soft and meek about Asher. He kissed just the same way he approached everything else in life, full throttle.

It didn't take long before Kennedy was gripping his

shoulders, holding tight because the room had begun to spin.

He nibbled and tasted. Teased and consumed. Conquered.

But Kennedy wasn't the kind to sit idly by and be taken. Pushing up onto her toes, she met him stroke for stroke, sucking his tongue and claiming pieces of him for herself.

He tasted like coffee and cinnamon. Smelled like sandalwood and the sea.

After several minutes, he broke away, staring at her out of glittering green eyes. Kennedy wanted to bask in the heat she saw there, revel in the power she'd wielded over him.

"We shouldn't be doing this," he finally said, his voice low and rough.

"Why not? We're both adults."

"You work for me. Your brother is my best friend. I'm worried this is going to become a problem at some point."

Kennedy let her hands play across his arms and shoulders, relishing the feel of his muscles and strength. "Jackson never has to know. In fact, for both our sakes, we need to make sure he never finds out. I work *with* you, not really for you, even if technically you are one of my bosses. Besides, that's only true for the next couple weeks."

Certain her assurance that whatever this was between them had a built-in expiration date would soothe the last of his reserve, she was startled when Asher pushed her away. She'd hoped he'd kiss her again, make her head and the room spin. Instead, cold air snaked across her almost naked body, sending goose bumps chasing over her skin.

But what he did next puzzled her even more. He tugged his shirt over his head, lifted it over her own and tugged it down her body. Inside out and backwards.

His warmth and scent enveloped her, making her even more discombobulated. "What are you doing?"

"I can't have this conversation with you standing in front of me half-naked. What do you mean that's only true for a couple more weeks?"

Uneasiness rolled through her belly, but Kennedy ignored it. She'd assumed Jackson would have already told Knox and Asher about her new job. She knew they usually stayed in regular contact no matter how far apart they were. But maybe, with everything going on in the Mediterranean, Jackson had forgotten to mention it. Or maybe he'd thought she'd tell Asher herself. She realized belatedly that would have been a good idea. Well, she could fill him in now.

She cleared her throat. "That call in the airport was a job offer from an advertising firm in Seattle."

"What?" Asher's voice was tight and controlled, but she could hear the anger pulsing just beneath the surface.

"I'll be leaving in about two weeks. It's a great opportunity and exactly the kind of position I went to school for."

"I didn't realize you were unhappy at Trident."

Kennedy frowned. "*Unhappy* is the wrong word. I like what I do."

"Then why are you leaving? Aren't we paying you enough? I'm sure Knox and Jackson would be happy to counter their offer."

She swallowed. How had this happened? They'd gone from half-naked to arguing intensely about her job. Somewhere along the way she'd missed the turn sign.

"Jackson already knows."

Asher went perfectly still. His gaze glittered dangerously. And every molecule of oxygen seemed to be sucked out of the air, his displeasure like a weight upon her skin.

"He what?"

"Jackson was aware I'd interviewed, and that there was a possibility I'd be leaving. I did promise to complete the documentary beforehand and help find a suitable replacement. I wouldn't disappear on you guys that way."

"You think that's my problem with the whole situation?"

"Well...yes. What else could you be upset about? So, your arguments about why this can't happen aren't valid. I've been around long enough to know you don't do long-term. It's perfect, really, since I'll only be here a couple more weeks. I want you."

She closed the gap between them, setting her hand against his naked chest. Her palm felt scorched from the heat of him, and an answering need throbbed right between her thighs.

Her other hand settled along the bulge of his erection, rubbing. A strangled hiss slipped through his clenched teeth. "And it's obvious you want me."

Kennedy didn't wait for his agreement but reached for the hem of the shirt he'd pulled over her head and tugged it off. Then she reached back to pop the catch on her bra. It fell to the ground between them.

Asher's gaze followed it, snagged on that taunting pile of cloth. Kennedy couldn't breathe.

Slowly, his eyes tracked up from the floor, over her calves and thighs, her hips and belly, bare breasts and tightened nipples.

When he reached her face, finally meeting her own stare, what she saw nearly had her running for the door. Because she was no longer confident she could handle this man.

Wild need, an unchecked drive for possession.

Asher wasn't the kind of man who did anything half-assed. He was intense, focused, thorough…

A shiver ricocheted through her body at the thought of that intensity pointed solely in her direction. Dangerous heat flared out from him, threatening to consume her.

"Give us both this," she managed to whisper. "No strings, no expectations. Just the next few days."

9

ASHER GROANED. HE was done. Couldn't walk away. And he knew it.

Kennedy stood there, legs spread, defiance in her eyes, and dared him to do his worst. The problem was, he wanted to give her only the best. Which wasn't smart, for either of them. Especially considering what she'd just told him.

Her words, *I'm leaving*, tied knots in his gut. They'd miss her at Trident, no doubt, but his reaction was more. And something he didn't want to dwell on. Especially not right now when Kennedy was naked before him, begging him with those tempting golden eyes to surrender to the physical need pulsing between them.

Asher stalked forward. Wrapping an arm around her waist, he brought her tight against his body, but kept going until her back connected with the wall of the room.

She gasped, the muted sound echoing through his head like a thunderclap. The soft swell of her breasts rose and fell against his hard chest.

Dipping his head, he found the curve of her neck

and licked. "I don't do forever, Kennedy," he whispered against her fragrant skin. She smelled like sugar and sin.

"Please." She laughed. "Retract that ego. You aren't the kind of man I could ever see myself with long-term, Asher. You're arrogant and dictatorial. Stubborn and insufferable."

"And you like boys you can bend to your will?"

"Not at all. Do I strike you as the kind of woman who prefers easy?"

"No." Kennedy didn't go looking for trouble, but she didn't shy away from hard topics, either. He admired the hell out of her tenacity and persistence. Even now, pressed against the wall and at his mercy, she was giving him attitude. And he liked it.

His mouth curved into an appreciative smile as he trailed his lips down her shoulder. His body raced with energy and excitement.

"It's sex, Ash, nothing more."

"Just so we're on the same page," he said, punctuating the statement with a playful bite of her shoulder.

She squeaked and then melted against him.

His hands roamed, touching as much of her as he could claim. Her skin was so smooth and silky. And he was damn well going to take his time and enjoy every second of this experience.

"Why the hell couldn't there be a bed?" he growled. He wanted to stretch her out and explore.

Kennedy scraped her fingernails lightly down his back, his skin tingling. Bringing her mouth to his chest, she trailed her tongue across his pec. And then paid him back by sinking her teeth into his shoulder. The bite was quick and didn't leave more than a momentary sting. It was the statement behind it that had his entire body revving. He could do anything he wanted, but she'd collect exactly what he got from her.

He didn't have to worry about her bending or breaking beneath the weight of his need. She could take whatever he dished out.

That was a heady thought.

Reaching between them, he yanked her panties down over her smooth thighs. Before he could even ask, she was stepping out of them, flicking a foot to send them sailing across the room.

She wanted this as much as he did.

Palming a thigh, he wrapped her leg around his hip and pressed against her.

Her dampness soaked into him through the barrier of his shorts. He needed that obstacle there to keep him in check. Without it, he would have simply sunk deep into her, uncaring about anything but the driving need to feel her wet heat wrapped around him. And she deserved better.

Reaching between them, Asher let his fingers play across her belly and hips. The crease of her thigh. Lightly dancing over the swell of her sex. Her hips arched, grinding tighter against him.

Finding her slippery with need, Asher groaned in the back of his throat. "Kennedy." He could just imagine how good it was going to feel to sheath himself inside the tight confines of her body.

Rolling her hips and chasing after his fingers, she said, "Touch me, Asher. Now. Right now."

How could he ignore such a sweetly implored order? Plunging one finger into her sex, Asher quickly realized that wasn't enough—for him or her.

He watched passion contort her features. Her head

dropped against the wall, but she didn't close her eyes. She watched him, that light brown gaze devouring his every move. There was something sexy about her direct stare, the way she didn't flinch or hide from what was happening between them.

She faced it head-on, accepting it for what it was. For a second, Asher felt a curl of jealousy. That kind of pragmatism must be liberating. He wanted to be able to look at the world and see it exactly the way it was. The way Kennedy saw it.

Plunging another finger deep inside her, Asher curled them and stroked, searching for the spot that would make her world shatter.

He knew the moment he found it. Her fingers tightened around his arms. Her eyelids flickered, going drowsy and heavy. Her breathing hitched. Her hips jerked. Her skin flushed a hot, beautiful pink.

"That's it, darlin'. Right there. I've got you," he murmured. In and out, over and over, he worked that single spot until she was panting and mindless. He added his thumb to her clit, gently rolling the bundle of nerves with just enough pressure to inflame but not send her over.

A dewy sheen that reminded him of heavy, humid summer nights back home slicked her skin. Leaning closer, he flicked his tongue over her collarbone, tasting salt and sex. Then he slipped down and sucked the tight bud of her breast deep into his mouth. The flavor of her burst across his tongue, and he wanted more.

He wanted to lap at her sex, drinking in everything she could give him as she writhed beneath the torment of his mouth.

Later.

Right now, he wanted to see her come.

"Please, Ash," she gasped, telling him she needed it almost as much as he did. He could practically feel the way her body throbbed. Or maybe that was his own pulse straining against the torturous band of his shorts. The same tempo was pounding at his temples, a rhythm taunting him to take.

Kennedy's hips moved against him, restless, needy. He could feel the muscles of her sex winding tighter, clamping down on his fingers. She trembled everywhere, her body so balanced on the edge that it wouldn't take much to send her over. God, he wanted that. To know he could bring her pleasure.

With several quick strokes, Asher sent her over. The orgasm ripped through her, and for a second it felt like the fury of it had claimed him, too. Her teeth sank into her bottom lip, trying to keep the keening cry locked inside her throat. What he wouldn't give to be somewhere truly private where he could make her scream over and over, each sound only for him.

She collapsed, sharing her weight with him and the wall at her back. Her fingers dug into him, as if she was afraid if she let up even a little she might slide to the floor.

Burying her face in the curve of his neck, her words caressed his skin. "Holy crap."

Pride and satisfaction ripped through him, mixing with the pounding desire that still rode him hard.

He barely had enough brainpower to grab the condom he always kept in his wallet before shedding his shorts. Somehow he managed to keep Kennedy upright at the same time, never losing his grip on her.

He was about to roll the condom over his erection when her hands covered his, stopping him.

"What?" he growled, for a second thinking she'd changed her mind. He should have known Kennedy wouldn't do that. She was many things, but a tease wasn't one.

Instead, she took the ring of latex from him, grinning with a smile that had restlessness and hunger mixing in his belly. Mischief and promise. In that moment he would have given just about anything to know the thoughts streaking through that diabolical and brilliant mind of hers.

Popping the condom into her mouth, Kennedy sank to her knees in front of him. This time, Asher didn't stop her. From beneath her lashes, she watched him.

Wrapping her hand around him, Kennedy leaned forward and used her lips and teeth to roll the condom down his hard shaft. The heat of her mouth was pure torture. Pressure. Perfection.

Asher pressed his palms to the wall, trying to keep himself upright. His knees felt like jelly as she stroked him, up and down, sucking hard and then barely touching him.

This was not how he wanted to come, but it felt so damn good.

Finally unable to take anymore, Asher grasped her and pulled her up. Spinning back to the desk, he'd never been so grateful for a cleared surface in his life.

Setting her on the edge, he spread her thighs wide and plunged deep inside. Kennedy groaned, arching her back and letting her head drop. She pushed up into each of his strokes, trying to get more.

God, could she be any more perfect?

Her body trembled against him. He could feel her winding hard for another orgasm and wanted it—for her and himself. He was greedy, craved everything she could give him.

Gritting his teeth, Asher pushed against his own orgasm, willfully holding out until he felt the first contractions of her release tighten around him. This time she buried her face against his chest, the muffled vibrations of her scream tearing through him right along with his own satisfaction.

He pushed through the tight fist of her sex, milking every moment of gratification for both of them. The world grayed out before imploding. His fingers dug into her hips, holding her still as his hips pumped in those last few long strokes.

When reality returned, they were both panting. Skin slick. Asher felt as if steam was rising off them.

Kennedy held on to him, and he wasn't sure if it was because she, like him, couldn't let go yet. Or because she was afraid she might end up on the floor. Not that he cared. He liked the way her arms wound tight around his waist.

"That was unbelievable," she finally said.

Asher nodded his agreement. It was. So damn good. Was that because it had been Kennedy or simply all the pent-up energy finally finding an outlet?

He really hoped it was the latter.

Trying to find some levity for both their sakes, Asher asked, "Where'd you learn to do that?"

Kennedy paused. He could feel the way her body stilled for a brief beat. "Do what?"

"That thing with the condom."

Her hands slipped up his back to his shoulders and pushed, putting space between them.

Eyes narrowed, she cocked her head to the side. "Putting it on with my mouth? Darlin'—" she imitated his accent "—that isn't even my best move."

Her hips undulated against him. For the first time Asher realized he was still buried deep inside her. And already starting to get hard. Damn. He shouldn't want her again so quickly. Not if this was just sex.

Especially not when she was going to be leaving.

Pulling out, he tied off the condom and tossed it in the trash. Then, desperately searching for even footing, he grabbed for the clothes scattered around the room—his and hers—and started putting his back on.

Kennedy watched him, slowly righting her own shirt and shorts. Her silent stare was unnerving. He had nothing to feel guilty about, yet he couldn't shake the prickle of it running down his back.

Wrapping a hand in her hair, Asher kissed her and then walked away.

It was an asshole move. He knew it, but couldn't stop himself from doing it anyway. Besides, maybe they both needed the reminder.

KENNEDY STARED ACROSS the deck at the hustle and bustle. The salvage crew had several divers down at the wreck site. Above, their safety coordinator was monitoring their progress through dive computers, video cameras attached to the salvage crew's dive suits and additional robotic cameras being operated from the deck. The production team had already requested access to their footage, which Trident had given…retaining the first right of refusal for usage in order to protect their proprietary information.

Alongside them, the preservation team worked on the pieces that had already been brought to the surface. Most of the more delicate work would be performed in labs either in the Bahamas or Jacksonville. But every piece had to be catalogued and documented, and steps were taken to prevent erosion due to exposure to the atmosphere after so much time beneath the water.

And in the midst of that normal chaos, the production team fluttered about.

The day was gorgeous, a perfect Caribbean morning with crystal clear skies and turquoise seas. The *Amphitrite* rocked beneath her feet, a steady movement that felt more like home than Kennedy would have ever anticipated. She didn't often get out of the office and into the field. Staring up at the bright blue sky, for the first time she realized she would miss this.

A hard band constricted around her chest, and her belly twisted uncomfortably. No, she wasn't having second thoughts about her decision to leave Trident. But there were plenty of things she loved about her job, and lately it had been challenging and exciting.

She loved the people she worked with, and getting to spend time with Jackson had become a major perk. She'd been twelve when he had left for the navy, and until he'd returned home for good, she'd only snagged snatches of time from his visits. The past two years she'd really gotten to know him as an adult and come to appreciate the man he was, not just love him because he was her brother.

Was she making a mistake? She'd watched her brother leave home and work hard to become an elite soldier. He'd protected his country and had the scars to prove it. There was a part of her that wanted to take those same risks with her own life, her own career. Surrounded by the safety net of her family and the certainty of her place within Trident, could she really reach her potential? Shouldn't she try to push herself outside that protective envelope?

A month ago Kennedy was certain of the answer. At the moment, not so much.

Today, the production team was filming the preservation crew working in the background as Asher described the painstaking process of retrieving artifacts and discussed the pieces already found—especially the captain's medal Avery had used to authenticate the wreckage. If they had enough good light later in the morning, they were hoping to get some shots with the dive team bringing up new pieces.

That had been on the agenda three days ago, but John's medical emergency had derailed them, something she'd heard Daniel grumbling about this morning. If she didn't know that John had been stabilized and was resting comfortably at the hospital in Nassau, she might think the man a major asshole. Okay, there was part of her that still thought it.

She understood that being down a cameraman made his job more difficult, but it wasn't like the man purposely had a heart attack. Apparently, they were going to keep him several days before allowing him to travel home with his wife and family. But John had many weeks of recovery ahead of him and a lifetime of bad habits to change.

Kennedy was just glad that his medical emergency wouldn't delay production, because even if she was feeling a bit nostalgic, she still needed the shoot to finish on time so she could pack her apartment and coordinate her move to Seattle.

Daniel wandered over to Asher and began explaining something to him. Kennedy should probably have been by Asher's side listening, as well. But she'd been avoiding him all morning.

The way he'd walked away from her after they'd made love had felt abrupt. He'd rocked her world, given her the most intense orgasm of her life and then just... disappeared.

She should have been ready for it. But the reality had stung more than she'd expected. And she really didn't want to investigate her reaction too deeply.

Kennedy was not used to men setting her off-kilter, which was something Asher had been doing from the first moment they'd met. That uneasiness had been part of the fireworks that sparked whenever they were close.

Now the heat they generated was just overwhelming, and she didn't trust herself near him until she had her own reactions firmly in hand. Honestly, she wasn't sure if she wanted to smack him or kiss him—not that she'd risk doing that where everyone could see.

But just the fact that her emotions were haywire told her she was in trouble. She could want him, but that was all.

So breathing room was a good idea.

But as she watched the team work, irritation settled deep inside her chest, building and building until she felt on the verge of exploding.

Although she wanted to avoid Asher, he was clearly avoiding her, too, which pissed her off. Maybe irrationally, but the burn was still there, licking through her chest.

Perhaps he'd gotten what he wanted and was now done with her.

It shouldn't surprise her. She'd seen him do the same thing to countless women over the time she'd known him. What had possessed her to think for one second that she was different?

Because she knew him? Because they worked together? Because he was her brother's friend?

Asher had been pretty specific about what she should expect. And she'd told him she wanted the same damn thing. Because she did!

She didn't want anything more than a repeat performance. But Asher...he didn't even seem as if he wanted that.

She'd barely had a chance to catch her breath before he was throwing clothes at her and walking out. Bar none, best sex of her life. And she wanted more. They were stuck on this boat together for several more days and she wasn't about to let him get away with this shit.

Throwing her hands on her hips, Kennedy stalked across the deck and pushed right between Asher and Daniel.

"Can I speak to you for a second?" she ground out.

Daniel threw her a startled expression, but she didn't have time to care about his reaction. Her gaze was trained solely on Asher.

"We're in the middle of something. Can it wait?"

"No, no it can't."

The more she looked at Asher, the more she remembered last night and thought about how he'd studiously ignored her this morning, the angrier she got. Now her emotions were bubbling way too close to the surface.

Kennedy realized her reaction wasn't entirely rational, but in the moment she couldn't do anything to regain a grasp on her temper. She didn't lose it often, but when she did…

What was it about this man that got under her skin? Everything with him was larger-than-life. He made her feel things…things she didn't want to deal with. Things that were perfectly inconvenient.

He made her feel more alive than she had in a very long time.

From the moment she'd met him, Asher had made her blood sing—with desire, annoyance…it didn't seem to matter.

"All right." Asher tossed Daniel an apologetic glance and then snagged her arm.

She'd started the confrontation—and there was no doubt this was going to be a confrontation—but the moment Asher's hand wrapped around her biceps it was evident he was the one in control.

Which should have pissed her off more, but just managed to add another explosive layer to the already combustible mix.

10

ASHER PROPELLED KENNEDY across the deck and into the quiet, dark hallway leading to the cabins.

"What the hell is wrong with you?"

"Wrong with *me*? Nothing, but you sure as hell are being an asshole and I'm not going to let it continue. We had sex, Asher. Damn good sex. So get over yourself and stop avoiding me. We have to work together, at least through the end of this project."

Irritation shot through Asher's system, burning and dangerous. He could feel it building inside, just looking for a target. Kennedy's eyes flashed, a wary glint that was a little too late. She took an instinctive step back.

Nope, that wasn't going to work. He'd tried to keep his distance, do the right thing, but she wasn't going to let him. Asher's hold on her arm tightened, preventing her from moving away.

"If I've been avoiding you it's for your own good."

"And was the way you ran away last night like your ass was on fire for my own good, as well? You're a whole host of things, Asher Reynolds, but one thing I never took you for was a coward."

A cold wave of dread and guilt swept through him. Part of him wanted to walk away again right now and save himself the complications that came with wanting Kennedy.

But he couldn't. Not when she was so close he could feel the heat of her seeping through to his skin. Not when her lush lips, thinned with anger, were just begging for him to take and taste. He wanted to give her another outlet for all that pent-up passion.

God, he just wanted her.

Tangling his fingers in Kennedy's hair, he angled her head and urged her up onto her toes so he could claim her mouth. The kiss was full of every speck of frustration, desire, heat and guilt he'd been fighting since walking away from her.

She groaned, the single sound like a cannonball, effective in demolishing every wall he'd tried to build back up between them.

"You have no idea how much I want to pull you into the nearest room, lock the door and taste every inch of you," he growled against her mouth. "But that's not a good idea, Kennedy. For either of us. I'm already in deep shit with your brother if he ever learns of this."

"I don't care what Jackson thinks."

"You might not, but I do. He's my best friend, Kennedy. My family. And I don't want to hurt or disappoint him."

"But you're perfectly willing to hurt and disappoint me?"

God, she knew just the words to say to send pain lancing through him.

"Of course not."

"Not since the night you bailed me out of jail has

anyone made me feel cheap, used and cast-off...until last night."

Her accusation cut deep, because he knew what it felt like to be discarded. But until that moment it had never occurred to him Kennedy might view his leaving in that same light.

His voice dipped down, going rough with regret. "That's the last thing I'd ever want to do, Kennedy. And I'm sorry if my actions made you feel less than treasured. What happened between us was amazing. Too amazing. I needed to get away from you. Find solid ground again."

A soft puff of laughter erupted through her kiss-swollen lips. "If you find it, please let me know, because I'm still floundering. Ash, I can't explain it. And I'd like to ignore it. But I can't. I'm not willing to walk away from this. At least not yet."

Those final words had uneasiness slithering through his belly, but not even that could banish his need for her. There was no way he'd be able to hold out, not when they were forced together on this ship for the next several days.

He was weak, and he'd had a taste. And not even worry over Jackson's reaction or concern that she was leaving in less than two weeks seemed to matter anymore.

At least he wasn't alone in the swirling maelstrom. It was obvious she was just as affected by what was happening between them as he was.

Giving in, Asher took several steps, crowding her against the wall of the walkway. His hands skimmed her sides, grasping her hips and pulling her tight against the ridge of his raging erection.

Kennedy sighed, the sound of surrender shooting straight through him as her body melted. He bit at her bottom lip, sucking it into his mouth. Her fingers dug into his shoulders, pulling him closer. She chased after him, twining their tongues together and pulling his deep into her own mouth.

Asher had no idea how long they stayed that way, pressed against the wall and kissing like teenagers. That was the way she made him feel, invincible and exuberant…and too stupid for his own good. Eventually, he was going to pay for this, but at the moment he didn't care.

After several minutes, Kennedy finally pulled away. Her voice was breathless when she said, "We need to stop. Anyone could walk in here and see us. The last thing we need is a rumor that we're together getting back to Jackson."

Her words made Asher feel as if he'd jumped from a helo straight into the coldest sea.

She wanted him, but didn't want anyone to know. And even if she was being logical, that still hurt. Her desire to hide what was happening between them poked at a place he'd thought long past healed, wounds his mother had inflicted and his ex-wife had cut deeper.

He wasn't good enough for anyone, maybe especially not Kennedy.

He'd walked away from her the night before, because he was afraid she was getting under his skin. Right now, he realized there was no avoiding the truth—she'd been there since the day they met.

And that scared him spitless, but there was nothing he could do about it. He had two choices—enjoy the time they had together or push her away and never look back.

He wasn't stupid. Leaning down, Asher found her mouth. He'd never been great with words, but with his body...

Electricity shot through him, sparking beneath his skin the moment their tongues met again. God, he needed to feel her beneath him. Needed an outlet for the energy and mixed up emotions threatening to overwhelm him. She met him stroke for stroke, as hungry for it as he was.

There was something gratifying and reassuring about realizing he wasn't alone in that need. Wrapping an arm around her back, Asher urged her close. "God, you're so damn soft," he groaned into her mouth.

She moaned, wrapped a leg around his waist for leverage and nipped at his bottom lip.

He cupped the back of her head with his palm, fingers caressing up and down the warm slope of her neck. Breaking free of her mouth, Asher set his lips there, trailing his tongue across her skin.

"Salty sweet," he murmured, greedy to take every bit of her while he could get it.

His hands swept down her body, searching for a way in through her clothes. He needed more of her. Right now.

But before he could even think about moving somewhere more private, Kennedy was pushing away from him.

Her eyes were bright, on fire, as she stared up at him, panting. Her skin was flushed pink. And her lips were swollen and wet.

His hands trembled. Actually trembled. He could feel

every molecule of his body straining toward her, searching, needing. He wasn't thinking about seduction but the demand to see, taste and touch everything about her.

Not just her body, skin, sex. Everything. He wanted her laughter, her sighs and her cries of pleasure. He wanted to know he could bring her those unbelievable moments. Wanted to make her orgasm over and over so that whenever another man touched her she would automatically think of him and how unbelievably he'd satisfied her.

What was it about Kennedy that had him losing every speck of finesse he'd ever possessed? Hell, he hadn't even been this way with Krista. Only Kennedy.

His arms were braced against the wall, caging her in. They both labored, trying to catch their breath. And he couldn't look away from her. Couldn't stop wanting her.

Finally, Kennedy stepped sideways, ducking beneath his arm. Asher started to follow, to pull her back into his arms, but she held out a single finger, shaking it back and forth.

"Nope. No more of that, sailor."

Asher growled.

"Daniel will be looking for us any moment. I'm surprised he isn't already bellowing."

So was he. As if on cue, a shadow fell between them, filling the doorway.

One of the production assistants stared at them, shifting his weight from foot to foot. "Everyone's waiting on deck,"

Closing the gap between himself and Kennedy, Asher slid his lips along the shell of her ear, issuing a promise and a warning. "This isn't finished."

SEVERAL HOURS LATER, exhaustion pulled at Kennedy's muscles. The day had been long, despite the fact that she'd done very little except watch the film crew work.

Daniel had decided it was time to head back into the office and rescheduled the question-and-answer session that had gone so terribly wrong the first night for tomorrow.

It hadn't taken a genius to realize Asher was nervous. Which meant they'd gone straight from a long day of shooting back to her room for a practice session…not exactly what she'd expected when Asher whispered that promise into her ear.

But the job came first. Asher needed her to be on her game and she needed the rest of filming to go smoothly.

They'd decided to go over the list of questions she'd prepared in anticipation of what Daniel might want him to discuss.

Kennedy assumed Asher's restless energy stemmed from concern over his fear of the camera and worry about his stutter.

Although she hadn't heard it in days, it had resurfaced the first time she'd asked him a question in front of the camera.

The tenser he became, the more pronounced the stutter. And she was getting frustrated, because she had no idea how to help him. Not really.

Rubbing a hand across her forehead, Kennedy looked down at the paper in her lap, reading off a question they'd covered more than once.

"Tell me the story of the *Chimera*."

"Sh-she went down in 1862."

Kennedy's gaze narrowed. The year was wrong, a

detail he'd already given her correctly several times. He was screwing with her on purpose now.

Fed up, Kennedy made an unhappy buzzing noise in the back of her throat. "Wrong. Thanks for playing. Fred, tell the man about his lovely parting gifts."

Asher's only reaction to her obnoxious behavior was a twitch at the corner of his mouth. "A hurricane brought her down in 1864, close to the end of the war."

So he did know the correct answer. "Where did she sail from?"

"Timbuktu."

This time, Kennedy grabbed one of the pillows piled behind her and aimed it right for his head. The infuriating man didn't even bother to duck. He simply snagged it out of the air and tossed it onto the floor at his feet.

"Keep it up, cupcake, and you won't have any place to lay your h-head tonight."

"Like I'm getting any sleep. At this rate we'll both be up all night."

He groaned, a pained expression crossing his face. "You're k-killing me, K-Kennedy."

Throwing the pages down onto the bed beside her, she raked him with a sharp gaze. "What do you want from me, Asher? I'm trying to help you here."

"What do I want? I've been fighting the urge to tip you back on that bed and rip every stitch of clothing off your body since we walked into this room. What I want is you."

Kennedy sucked in a harsh breath, her entire body suffusing with a combustible heat that burned from the inside out. As if she'd been dormant, just waiting for some word or sign from him to ignite.

"You want to see me naked? Fine. For every question you get right, I lose an item of clothing."

Interest sharpened his gaze. He tipped his head sideways, considering her for several seconds. "What if I get one wrong?"

"I put something back on."

A deep, dark sound vibrated through Asher's chest. His gaze went white-hot. "I'm going to hell," he breathed out.

11

LAUGHTER BUBBLED UP inside of Kennedy, an unexpected sensation mixing with the fire running through her veins. "Because you want me? I don't think so."

"Because I damn well know better, but when you're close it doesn't seem to matter. You get under my skin."

"Nice to know I'm not the only one affected."

A gush of laughter flowed past his lips. "Hardly."

Slipping up onto her knees, Kennedy pulled the stack of papers back in front of her. "Business before pleasure."

She was really going to do this, play a bastardized version of strip poker with Asher Reynolds, her naked body as the prize. Shaking her head, she pushed the last of her qualms away.

"Tell me about my family's history with the *Chimera*."

"You and Jackson were raised on stories of the ship. Not what the historians believed, but the real story. Your ancestor was one of the owners, aboard when she sank. He'd traveled to several plantations in the Caribbean gathering supplies, support and a secret stash of gold for the Confederacy. Jackson spent years tracing the route the *Chimera* took, looking for any obscure historical mention of her, the crew or her cargo."

"Good boy." Kennedy grinned at him. Reaching for the hem of her shirt, she dragged it up her torso. The feel of her own fingers against her skin was soft and subtle. The zing came from knowing that Asher's eyes traced the same path, devouring each inch of skin she revealed.

She could feel him watching her with that preternatural intensity that stirred her blood.

Yanking the cotton off over her head, she tossed it on to the floor between them. It landed with a muted *swish*, but it felt as if the sound echoed through the tiny room.

She wanted him to touch her, but he didn't move. He swallowed, the muscles in his thick throat flexing.

"Keep going," she finally said, her voice low and breathy.

"After Loralei's father stole Jackson's research."

Kennedy shook her head, making a low, disapproving sound in the back of her throat.

"No, we don't want to mention anything about Loralei's father stealing from Trident. Lancaster is our partner now. That's history between us and not for public consumption."

She made a move to climb off the bed and retrieve the shirt she'd just thrown down, so that she could put it back on, but Asher beat her to it.

His boot-clad foot landed on top of it, pinning the cotton to the floor.

"No."

"That was the agreement."

"I'm changing it."

Reaching for the bottom of his own T-shirt, Asher whipped it off in less than half a second.

"I screw up, I take something off instead."

"That's hardly an incentive for you to keep getting things right."

Bending at the waist, Asher scooped her shirt up and tucked it beneath his right hip. "Cupcake, the only way you're getting this back right now is by taking it from me. Do you really think you can do that?"

Kennedy narrowed her gaze. He was taller than her, had probably a hundred pounds of muscle on her and years of elite tactical training. She wasn't stupid. Although, there were ways to bring a man like him to his knees. And she wasn't above fighting dirty if she needed to.

But, as she stared at the ripple of his abs and the rounded curve of his defined pecs, she had to wonder. Did she really want to argue with him?

Not particularly.

"Fine."

"So, what's the official statement on Lancaster Diving?"

"We partnered together, Jackson consulting with a friend in the industry."

"Lancaster was no friend," Asher groused.

"I'm aware of that, and so is everyone else who matters. This is to protect Trident."

"No, this is to protect Loralei."

"Considering she and Jackson are on the verge of getting married, that's pretty much the same thing, don't you think?"

She watched as a muscle in Asher's jaw ticked for a few minutes before he finally took a deep breath.

"Fine. The asshole is dead, and Loralei is a good woman," he said.

"Exactly."

"But it bothers me that we're hiding the truth. That doesn't sit well."

"Noted."

For some reason, Kennedy was surprised at his stance. As a member of Special Forces, surely he'd had to lie before. There was a part of her that wanted to ask the question, but was afraid to. Not only because she wasn't certain she wanted the answer, but also because they didn't have the luxury of time to get off track.

"I won't lie, but I won't bring up something we want to keep quiet, either. That's the best I can give you."

It wasn't ideal, but she'd take it. And stay close during the interview tomorrow, so she could intervene if it looked like things were going to get sticky.

"Fair enough."

"Loralei researched the historical hurricane records, matching the track of the storm with the projected path of the *Chimera*. After discovering that a group of plantation owners had purchased the *Chimera* quietly, she began to cross-reference their locations with the storm, coming up with a small island no one had thought to check. That information, paired with what Jackson had, led them both to the *Chimera*'s resting place."

Asher paused, cocked an eyebrow and waited.

Shifting back onto her rear, Kennedy cursed the tropical location and the decided lack of wardrobe pieces the climate required. Why couldn't she have been wearing socks and several layers?

Unbuttoning her shorts, she shimmied out of them,

letting them dangle from the end of her foot before dropping them onto the floor.

Asher snatched them up as well, tossing them onto the desk behind him.

"Spread your thighs for me, angel."

The muscles in her legs clenched, an instinctive search for relief from the pressure building at her core. She thought about refusing, but realized she didn't want to.

She wanted him to look at her. To see just how turned on she was. For him.

Scooting back to the center of the bed, Kennedy rose onto her knees. Spreading them wide, she sank until the curve of her ass touched her heels.

Gratification came in the form of Asher's rushed breath.

"You weren't lying. I can see your panties are damp from here." His hot gaze dragged up her body, zeroing in on her face. "Do you have any idea how much I want you right now? It's taking everything I have to sit here."

Satisfaction and power swirled inside her. There was something decidedly wicked and energizing about realizing she could make this man, who was known for his flippant attitude and tight control, get so close to the edge of losing it.

"Tell me more."

"I want to rip those panties off you and plunge my tongue deep inside. I want to taste you, lick up every drop of your arousal."

Kennedy swallowed. Her sex throbbed. She wanted that, too.

"I meant about the *Chimera*," she managed to croak.

A devilish grin twisted Asher's lips. If she knew her

effect on him, he was wholly aware of his effect on her. And wasn't above using it against her.

He placed a hand on his chest and ran his fingers across his pecs and down over his abs. Her palms twitched. She wanted to be the one touching him.

Her nipples tightened, aching, as if he was touching her and not himself.

Kennedy shifted, intent on bringing her thighs together so she could rub some relief.

"Don't," he said, the single word arrogant and commanding. "Stay right there."

She couldn't breathe. Her lungs had stopped working, only able to pull in shallow gulps of air. She watched Asher's hand move lower, flicking at the buttons on the fly of his khakis.

"You haven't missed a question," she managed to force past her dry throat.

"Who said I'm taking these off? I just don't want a permanent imprint of the buttons on my dick."

Spreading the fly wide, he might as well have pulled the pants all the way off. His erection strained against the dark gray boxer-briefs beneath, hiding not a damn thing. She could see the spreading wet spot where the head of his cock pressed against the tight waistband.

She couldn't help herself. Her tongue licked across her lips. He wasn't the only one who wanted a taste. She was desperate to pull the long length of him into her mouth and suck. Hard. She craved the sounds of pleasure he'd make when she took him deep.

"You keep looking at me like that, and you're going to get exactly what you want."

Kennedy's gaze jerked back up to his. "What do I want?"

"Me buried between those soft pink lips."

He wasn't wrong. But two could play at this game.

Reaching up, Kennedy slipped a single finger into her open mouth, dragging her tongue across the surface as she pulled it back out again.

Asher's green eyes flashed. A burst of electricity erupted across her skin. "That's playing dirty."

She shrugged. "All's fair in love and strip-tease games?"

Jeez, the room had gotten muggy. Sweat that had nothing to do with the tropical location pearled up beneath her hair and down her back.

Her thighs trembled, from kneeling and from need. But she didn't want whatever this was to stop, so she stayed right where she was.

The way Asher watched her…she felt both beautiful and desired. Wanted and needed.

"Several months after Jackson and Loralie discovered the wreck, the salvage hit a snag when Anderson McNair made a claim that she was not the *Chimera*. Trident brought Avery Walsh on board to authenticate the wreckage. After a close call with some drug runners and explosives, we discovered that McNair's diving company was a front for drug smuggling, and the wreckage sat smack in the middle of his drop zone."

It took Kennedy several seconds for her brain to catch up to what Asher was saying. Oh, yeah, they were preparing for tomorrow's shoot by going over details.

Another couple of seconds to realize he'd gone off on another tangent. "Nope, can't talk about that either."

"Why the hell not? The whole damn world knows this part of the story. It played out on national television in the middle of a press conference."

"Not completely. Besides, we've been asked to keep any information we have private, since the trial for Mc-Nair's associates is still pending."

"Hell, cupcake, you don't want any of the juicy, fun stuff to come out, do you?"

"Not my decision."

"What's left to talk about?"

"How about Avery's discovery of a medal that she used to tie the captain to the ship? It's the little details that can sometimes make the biggest impact."

"You mean like how your skin flushes pink beneath that honey tone when you're turned on?"

The man had the ability to knock her on her ass with just a few words. Every time she thought she had her footing firmly back in place, he said something to send her reeling again.

"Yes. Like that."

"I think it's time for you to lose another piece of clothing, Kennedy." Asher's voice dipped down into that dangerous register, the one that made goose bumps spread across her skin.

"I don't think so. You got that one wrong."

"No, I got it right, you just don't want me to tell the truth. Again."

Kennedy sighed.

"How about we compromise and both lose something?"

She did want to see those strong thighs and his tight ass. And her bra was chaffing at her nipples anyway. "Fine. But you first."

Asher flashed her a brilliantly deviant grin and stood. Easing his hands into the already open waistband, he pushed and crouched low. It was a constant amazement to her, how smoothly the large man could move.

When he rose, the pants stayed pooled on the ground. His thighs flared out, the cut of muscle there making her mouth go dry. She wanted to run her tongue up the long, lean line.

And his ass. From here she could see the way his glutes indented on the sides. Was it bad that she wanted to take a bite out of him?

Probably.

Collapsing back into the chair, Asher didn't bother to hide the little that was still covered by his briefs. He sprawled back, legs wide, massive erection straining against the band of spandex and cotton.

"Your turn."

Reaching behind her, Kennedy unsnapped the tiny clasps holding the satin and lace against her body. She pulled in a deep breath the moment they released and let it out on a sigh of relief. The straps slipped down her shoulders, but an arm across her chest held the material in place.

Settling back onto her heels again, Kennedy watched him. Studied the way his gaze devoured her.

Slowly, she let go, her bra dropping onto the bed in front of her.

His tongue swiped across his lips. She wanted him to lick her. Kiss her. Tug at her throbbing nipples with the tips of his teeth. To make her writhe beneath him, in the way only Asher could.

She'd had lovers, more than a handful over the years. But none of them had ever looked at her like Asher did. As if his entire world had condensed down to the two of them. Together.

There was no question why he never had any problems filling his bed. He was gorgeous, intense, a little dangerous and completely involved with whomever was in front of him.

Tonight, that was her. And she was going to take every moment she could get.

"Soft pink." His gaze found hers. "You have the most amazing breasts, Kennedy. A perfect handful. And your nipples are so damn responsive. I bet I could make you come just by sucking on them."

At the moment, she wasn't entirely certain he couldn't make her come just by talking to her like that.

Suddenly, Asher surged out of the chair. It crashed back against the desk before tipping onto its side. Neither of them seemed to care.

"I'm done with this game," he said, stalking closer.

Kennedy instinctively scrambled backward on the bed, but she didn't get far. His arms came around her, pulling her up onto her knees and crushing her against the hard wall of his chest.

She was suddenly apprehensive. Not about him touching her. But about her ability to keep her own emotions in check. She'd spent the past two years thinking she didn't particularly like this man.

She'd been lying—to him and herself.

If they'd simply started going at each other again, like yesterday, it might have been different. Her defenses might have remained in place.

Unfortunately, they were in tatters at her feet, mixed in with the pile of their clothing. She felt more exposed, and it had nothing to do with being almost naked.

But he didn't give her a chance to get back on even ground. Instead, he tore away the last barriers between them. With a twist of his fingers, he ripped through the tiny strings across her hips and left her panties in a frayed pile on the bed.

His own shorts disappeared, and they were skin on skin. Burning heat to burning heat.

God, he smelled so damn good. Man and musk with a hint of salt and sunshine from being above deck all day.

Her mouth found his neck, licking and sucking. Taking a nipping bite of him, because she wanted a piece of him if he was going to steal a piece of her.

His fingers weren't rough, but insistent, as they traveled across her body. He plucked at her nipples, flicking them. Kennedy arched up, asking for more.

His mouth found her, sucking hard and pulling a cry from her parted lips before changing up and laving her softly. The constant push and pull had her head spinning.

Her hands gripped his ass, trying to pull him closer.

"God, Ash, I need... I need," she panted out, completely gone.

"I know, angel," he whispered into her ear, his hands sweeping across her temples, tangling into her hair.

She writhed beneath him, searching. Her hands found the hard length of his sex. She couldn't keep a sound of satisfaction from vibrating through her throat when she closed a fist around him and started pumping.

He hissed, his hips bumping against her in rhythm.

"I want you in my mouth," she murmured against him, satisfying herself with sucking his bottom lip since she couldn't wiggle down far enough to get to him.

"Later."

Hooking an arm beneath the bend in her knee, Asher

pressed, opening her wide. She should have felt pinned beneath him, but she didn't. In that moment, it felt as if the weight of his body was the only thing holding her to the earth.

His fingers found the slippery folds of her sex. She whimpered. He rubbed at her clit, around it, over it, circling close and then slipping away again. Torturing her in a way that made the world go black.

Or maybe that was just because she closed her eyes, unable to deal with the intensity of what he was making her feel.

He stopped briefly. She heard foil tearing and realized he'd gotten a condom from somewhere. "Thank you," she managed to breathe out.

Asher didn't pretend not to understand what she meant. "I'll always take care of you."

It was a promise she believed. At least in that moment. Asher had always been there for her when she'd needed him.

That was the last thought she had before she felt the head of his cock pressing against the tight opening of her sex. He eased in, inch by glorious inch, sinking slowly.

She didn't want slow. Kennedy needed fast and hard. Unbridled.

Gripping the curve of his ass, she pushed down at the same time she surged up. He entered her fully with that one fluid thrust.

Asher cursed against her lips before claiming her mouth and pinning her hips tight to the bed so that she couldn't move.

"Minx," he growled a few seconds later, pulling back. "That wasn't for you. That was for me. I'm trying not to go off like a teenager, but you feel so damn good. I'm gonna lose it."

Kennedy stared up at him, taking in the brilliant light in his green eyes. "I want you to lose it. Give it to me, Ash. Don't hold back."

If she couldn't, she didn't want him to, either. She needed him lost in the storm of sensation with her.

Rearing up, she sealed her mouth to his, sweeping her tongue deep inside. And he gave her exactly what she'd asked for.

His hands touched her everywhere. His mouth and tongue teased her neck, ear, shoulder. All the while, he moved with a steady pace, hitting that perfect spot deep inside that had sparks sputtering through her blood.

"Ash, I'm gonna…" She couldn't even get the words out.

"I've got you, darlin'"

Her mouth opened on a silent cry that suddenly wasn't silent at all. Words spilled from her mouth, although she couldn't say what they were. But Asher caught each one, smothering the sound with his own lips and taking them for himself.

Her entire body exploded, and the waves of pleasure just kept going. Her hips surged, chasing the ecstasy that only Asher could give her.

And then every muscle in her body collapsed beneath the weight of relief. A few seconds later a shudder raced down his spine. Kennedy ran her hands over his back and shoulders, wanting to feel the physical evidence of his desire for her.

She felt the kick of him deep inside, her own body clenching hard around him. Asher buried his face in her shoulder, muffling the cry of his orgasm. But she felt the vibration of it. Relished it.

And wanted it again.

Even after that unbelievable explosion she needed more of him.

And that scared her. But not enough to move. And certainly not enough to push him away.

12

It FELT LIKE déjà vu, standing at the back of the room watching the production team scurry around Asher. He was even wearing the same clothes—the slacks and shirt with the sleeves rolled up and the top two buttons undone.

The difference was that now she was intimately familiar with the body hidden beneath. And she was finding it difficult not to fantasize, stuck here in her little corner. Which wasn't the best considering she was pretty sure Asher was close to a meltdown. Not that anyone else would notice.

He looked amazing, and she was struggling not to cross the room and put her lips just where his shirt revealed that tender place on his neck, so the taste of his skin could flood her mouth once more.

But there were too many prying eyes for that kind of behavior. They'd already been pushing their luck. Eventually, word was going to get back to Jackson that something between the two of them had changed. And she didn't want that.

Jackson would get upset—because he was her overprotective big brother. Which wouldn't be fair to Asher. She didn't want to be the source of tension between the men, especially since in a handful of days she'd be leaving.

She realized now, more than ever, how important Jackson, Knox and the Trident family were to Asher. He'd lost so much—his father, mother, grandmother, wife…she refused to be the cause of him losing anything more.

So, Kennedy stayed in the background, her own belly full of sympathetic butterflies, and kept her gaze trained on Asher.

To anyone else who was watching him, he would appear perfectly calm and in control. But over the past few days Kennedy had become intimately familiar with him, and she could see the signs of strain.

The tick of a muscle right below his jaw. The tension tightening around his eyes. The way his fingers curled into the edge of the desk. The single-syllable words he used to answer the production crew's questions.

Kennedy was fully aware of what was at stake today and just how badly this moment could go. And she needed to figure out some way to get him to relax or this shoot was going to end in disaster.

Crossing the room, she pushed her way between Carmen and one of the production assistants, throwing them both megawatt smiles.

"Could you guys give us a minute?"

Everyone around them backed away, giving them a few feet of space. It wasn't much to work with, but it would have to do.

Conscious of multiple pairs of eyes on them, Kennedy was careful when she casually rested her hands on Asher's knees.

Pitching her voice low, she said, "Hey, frogman, how ya' doing?"

"Fine." His mouth was thin. His voice tight.

"You can bullshit everyone else in this room, Asher Reynolds, but don't try to pull that with me. You're not fine, and that's okay. The world isn't going to end because you aren't perfect."

His mouth twisted, but a brief flash of humor lit up his gaze. She'd take it.

Leaning forward, Asher murmured, "I don't suppose there's any way I could convince you to leave?"

Kennedy's brows creased with confusion. "Why would I leave?"

"Because you make me nervous, cupcake, and I'm already nervous enough."

The laughter that bubbled out was unintended. She didn't even know it was coming until it was too late to stop it. But it had a surprising effect—an answering lightness spread across Asher's expression. His body relaxed, most of the tension leaking away and leaving behind the strong, intelligent, competent man she'd come to know.

"I'm your friend, Asher. I'm on your side and should be the least of your worries."

"I don't want to look like an idiot in front of you."

His confession was endearing, especially since a few weeks ago she hadn't thought he gave a damn how she felt about anything, much less him.

"Well, then let me put your mind at ease. You could screw this up royally, Asher, and it wouldn't change my opinion of you one iota. You're a damn good businessman, an unbelievable friend to my brother and someone who's risked his life to protect this country. I have faith in your ability to do this. Now you need to have faith in yourself."

Asher merely blinked at her. She wasn't sure if her words had stunned him or if he didn't have anything to say.

"But, just in case you need a little incentive, I'm not above rewarding excellent work." Kennedy tossed him a saucy wink and then walked away.

Looking back over her shoulder, she noticed the wicked grin spreading across Asher's face. Her belly dropped as if she'd just ridden the world's fastest roller coaster. She'd always liked roller coasters.

Taking her spot in the back corner again, she didn't notice Daniel until he was standing right beside her.

"I have no idea what you just said to him, but thanks. I was getting seriously worried."

Kennedy shrugged her shoulders. "No problem. He gets a little uptight and nervous in front of the camera, that's all. He's a perfectionist in everything and is worried he's going to screw up the entire production. The trick is to get him concentrating on something else so he doesn't become a self-fulfilling prophecy of doom."

Daniel chuckled. "I'll remember that. You have a knack for this, you know."

Kennedy couldn't stop the flood of pride and accomplishment, or the way she soaked in his praise. It was nice to have her hard work acknowledged, especially considering the hurdles they'd had to overcome so far and the fact that Daniel hadn't exactly been a breeze to work with.

Maybe moving to Seattle wasn't a bad idea after all.

With Masters, Dillon and Cooper she'd have the opportunity to work on major ad campaigns, including interacting with television, magazine and radio outlets. She'd get to use the skills she was honing here.

Her gaze landed on Asher and her belly twisted again, only this time it wasn't with giddy excitement.

But she didn't have time to examine her reaction because Daniel moved away, shouting, "Quiet, everyone! Asher, are you ready?"

The room went still. Beside her, one of the cameras buzzed faintly, and her body forgot how to breathe.

She waited, because even she wasn't entirely certain what was about to happen.

ASHER HEARD DANIEL yell action, and for a minute thought he might throw up. The calm he'd felt with Kennedy had completely disappeared. The familiar pressure was back, pushing against his lungs and strangling his throat. His tongue felt swollen, thick and useless.

He could already imagine everyone's reaction as he stumbled over the first word he tried to force through his mouth.

God, this was a nightmare. His nightmare.

Jackson and Knox were depending on him. Trident needed this documentary for the exposure, the revenue and the potential to increase their clientele.

And he was going to let everyone down. He could feel the panic, the grief and the guilt that always swirled together whenever he stuttered.

Then he found Kennedy in the crowd and his entire world seemed to shift back into place. The pressure eased. The stranglehold on his throat disappeared and a cleansing swell of air filled his lungs.

He expected to see her eyes full of wary concern, but they weren't. She stared back at him, steady, expectant and confident that he could handle this without a problem.

And that was exactly what he needed, that shot of strength when he thought he didn't have enough of his own to conquer his irrational fear.

"Asher, why don't you start with some background on Trident? How did you, Jackson and Knox form the business?"

Kennedy nodded her encouragement. Asher opened his mouth and words flowed out. "At first, the idea of forming Trident Diving and Salvage was little more than a fantasy, as outlandish as the idea that three former navy SEALs could uncover a one-hundred-and-fifty-year-old ship that seasoned experts hadn't been able to find. I c-c-can't—"

The stutter came out of nowhere, startling him as much as everyone else in the room. Asher froze for several seconds, his gaze flashing back to Kennedy.

And she was there, that same steady, expectant, accepting gaze still unwavering as she waited for him to continue.

She really had meant it when she'd said it didn't matter.

So Asher took a deep breath and just kept going. "I can't even remember which one of us said it first. For two years we listened to Jackson Duchane talk about the *Chimera* with awe in his voice like she was more important than the Holy Grail."

Asher laughed, the memories of those days flooding back. They weren't all good, but they weren't all bad. Sitting in some shithole outside a small mud hut in Afghanistan. Or around a campfire in the middle of the jungle in Central America. Or even relaxing in the backyard with steaks on the barbecue and a beer in their hands whenever they'd been home.

Somehow Jackson had always managed to bring the topic around to the *Chimera*. Before he'd met Loralei, that ship had been his life.

"I'm just lucky Jackson let me become a part of the team, the family we've built. The *Chimera* is important, she's historically valuable and will be key in uncovering new information about the support the Confederacy received from the Caribbean plantation owners. But for me, this experience has been more than that. I'll always be grateful for the brothers I met in combat and the life we've built together now that we've all moved to the next chapter of our lives."

Asher realized that he'd been talking for several minutes, rambling on in a way he hadn't meant to, giving Daniel information that had nothing to do with the purpose of the documentary. Finding Daniel in the shadows behind the camera, he offered an apologetic smile. "Sorry, I didn't mean to drone on. And can we redo that first part, where I stuttered?"

"No."

Shit. That single-word answer had Asher's stomach rolling with dread. Daniel was pissed.

"That take was perfect, there's no need to reshoot it. We can edit out the stutter. Do you need a break or would you like to continue?"

Asher shook his head, a little shocked and unnerved. "A break would be nice." His fingers were cramping where he'd had a death grip on the edge of the desk anyway.

"Take five, everyone!" Daniel yelled before turning to Kennedy. And for everyone in the crew to hear, he said, "You were right. He's perfect. America is going to eat him up."

Kennedy grinned. "I'll remind you of that later when you're upset with me over something else."

"I don't doubt it."

Pushing away from the wall, Kennedy slowly strode across the room. People moved around, adjusting equipment, speaking to each other. None of that really registered because he couldn't pull his eyes away from her.

She stopped several inches away, a hell of a lot farther than he would have preferred, cocked her head to the side and stared up at him for several seconds before murmuring, "I'm so proud of you."

Until that moment, he hadn't realized just how important hearing that from her would be. Pride burned through him, easing years of scars he hadn't realized he was still carrying.

"Thank you," he murmured back. Leaning forward, he got as close to her as he could without actually touching, not caring who was watching. In that moment, nothing else mattered but her. "Now, about that reward you mentioned…"

13

"Mmm," Asher hummed in the back of his throat. The sweet scent of vanilla tickled his senses. Something soft brushed across his parted lips.

Cracking one eye open, he stared up at Kennedy looming out of the darkness above him.

Her thighs were spread on either side of his hips. Slowly, she rocked, dragging another sound of pleasure from him as her wet sex slid against his already throbbing erection.

"I could get used to waking up to this," he rumbled, threading his fingers through her hair and pulling her down closer. He wanted to taste her, but before he could, something soft and wet swept across his cheek.

The sensation startled him. It wasn't her tongue because her mouth was inches away from his. "What the hell?"

A wicked grin crossed her face. Kennedy placed a palm on his chest and levered herself up, putting a few inches between them. And for the first time he realized she held something in her other hand.

A pale cupcake with a swirl of bright pink frosting at least two inches thick.

Eyeing it, he asked, "What is that?"

Her grin widened. "Payback."

Before he could even twitch, the thing was top down in his face. Kennedy smeared the sticky mess from his forehead, down his nose and across his chin.

There was no question, he was under siege.

Ducking his head, Asher grabbed her by the waist, picked her up and flipped her onto her back. But the damage was already done.

She squealed and giggled, the sound making his chest go tight for several seconds. It was playful. It was real. He liked knowing he could make Kennedy laugh.

She was driven and focused. Watching her the past two years, he'd noticed she tended to shoulder responsibility, taking on tasks simply because she could. The woman was in constant motion, and she rarely took a break long enough to relax.

At least not since the night he'd rescued her from jail.

If she dated, he wasn't aware of it. Her entire life had been focused on helping them build Trident while completing her degree.

He commended her for the dedication, but being a soldier had quickly taught him the necessity of blowing off steam. If you didn't open the release valve now and then, stress would eat you up from the inside out.

So if Kennedy wanted to smear him in a little pink frosting for fun…they'd both enjoy licking up the mess.

But he wasn't about to make it easy for her.

Using his legs, Asher pinned her thighs down beneath him. But he wasn't quick enough to avoid another smear of sugary goodness across his chest.

With one hand, he captured her wrist, holding her arm above her head and immobilizing her weapon of choice.

Asher sucked in a harsh breath when she arched beneath him, the tight tips of her breasts colliding with his chest. Her hips slid against his. Naked wrestling definitely put him at a disadvantage. At least when his opponent was Kennedy.

His brain fogged for a few seconds, and she managed to grab another cupcake from a plate she'd set beside the bed. If he hadn't been distracted, she never would have reached the additional ammo.

She hadn't just brought one, but a full dozen of the sticky pink things.

"How did you get these?" he managed to get out, even while attempting to pin her free hand.

"Catherine made them after she was done fixing the crew dinner," she answered, taking a huge bite before smearing the top of the cupcake across his ribs.

"Remind me to thank her," he growled right before burying his face against Kennedy's neck. The way her breath caught as he dragged his tongue over her skin sent a hot stream of molten need straight to his blood.

Making a calculated decision, Asher didn't bother to snag her other wrist, but let her continue spreading the stickiness over his body.

Stretching out, he grabbed some ammunition of his own and struck. She yelped in surprise, bucking her hips beneath him to try and wiggle away. But he had her well and truly pinned.

"Nowhere to go, sugar," he drawled.

Pushing against him, she glared up. But her golden

brown eyes twinkled. "Sugar isn't any better than cupcake, you Southern-fried Neanderthal."

Dipping his finger in the pink confection, Asher spread a smear across Kennedy's chest, collarbone to collarbone. And then dipped his head down to nibble and lick his way along the same path.

Her fingers tightened on his shoulder, not to push him away again, but to pull him closer.

"I only use nicknames with people I actually like," he murmured against her skin.

She sighed and squirmed, her hand dropping uselessly to the bed, cupcake completely forgotten. "Why cupcake? It sounds so…"

"Sweet."

"Empty-headed and pointless."

He chuckled. "Hardly. Those are two terms I'd never use to describe you." Pushing up on to his elbows, Asher abandoned his own cupcake, threading his fingers through the loose curls of her silky blond hair. For several seconds he gazed at her, his heart thumping erratically inside his chest. As though he was about to make a HALO jump.

He smoothed several strands away from her face before answering. "Cupcake is the perfect description for you, Kennedy. The kind of treat you know you shouldn't want, but you can't seem to stop craving."

Her lips parted. A soft sound escaped, but he wasn't sure what it meant. Her eyes flashed bright for several seconds before going dark again.

He seriously needed to lighten this up.

"Besides, I always knew you'd be so damn sweet to taste." Lowering his head, Asher pulled the pebbled tip of her breast deep into his mouth.

He wasn't wrong. Above everything else he could taste the overpowering sweetness of the sugary buttercream. But beneath that was all Kennedy. Vanilla and spice and something soft and sensual. That flavor was more addictive than anything he'd ever encountered.

And had the potential to be a hell of a lot worse for him than eating an entire plate of cupcakes.

She arched into his caress, offering him more. But she wasn't content to merely receive. She wanted to take and give, as well.

The hot point of her tongue scraped against his shoulder over his chest and up his neck. She sucked and nibbled, lapping up every speck of icing she could find.

By the time she wiggled down to get the spots across his ribs, Asher was panting from how good it felt to have her touch him.

Sex had never been this fun or sizzling with anyone else.

What was it about Kennedy that made him feel as if they'd been together like this forever? That he knew her inside and out…and she knew him?

Maybe it was the fact that they'd worked together, knew each other outside the bedroom, but he really didn't think so.

This was more than simple familiarity.

There was a connection, an understanding that had always stretched between them.

It both thrilled and terrified him. And that was the real reason he'd kept Kennedy at arm's length all this time. Instinctively, he'd known she could become important.

But that wasn't an option. Not when she was Jackson's little sister. Not when every relationship in his life had ended in miserable failure. Not when even his own mother hadn't thought him worthy of her time and love.

Not when she would walk away in less than two weeks.

What was it about him that was drawn to women who wouldn't stay? Why did he always fall for them, even though he knew better?

Right now, he was too far gone to search for answers or find the elusive distance he'd been fighting to maintain. How could he possibly find it with Kennedy writhing and moaning beneath him?

They came together in a tangled mass of hands, tongues, mouths and whispered sighs. Last night had been a frenzy. In the early morning hours before the rest of the world awoke, they discovered a kind of blissful, easy, vivid peace.

Their skin stuck together in places. Tiny grains of sugar coated them both. But none of that mattered.

One minute they were apart and the next Asher, sheathed in a condom, was buried deep inside her. Kennedy's hiss of satisfaction rushed across his skin. She gripped him hard, her hands trying to coax him into defying physics to bring them closer.

And maybe he could.

With slow, steady thrusts, Asher let the bliss build.

"God, you feel amazing," he rumbled before sucking the speeding pulse at her throat into his mouth.

He could feel the way she spiraled up, her body tightening beneath him as they both barreled headlong into ecstasy. Her muscles clamped hard around him, squeezing and tempting him into letting go. But he wasn't ready for this to be over yet.

He was greedy and wanted every second of Kennedy he could get, especially since those moments were numbered.

Her panted breaths became whimpers of need, sweet music to his ears. He loved knowing he could make her feel that kind of pleasure.

"Ash, please. Please," she begged.

"That's it, angel. Let go."

Her orgasm crashed over them both. Asher smothered her cry with a soul-deep kiss. The force of it was too much for him. The ball of fire built at the small of his back, exploding out in wave after wave of intoxicating pleasure.

Together, they collapsed onto the bed. Asher rolled them both until Kennedy was tucked at his side, her head lodged beneath his chin.

Closing his eyes, he tried to regain…something. His equilibrium, his sanity, his autonomy. He wasn't sure, just that the woman in his arms had devastated him… in the best way possible.

They lay like that for several minutes. Slowly, awareness returned. Asher was pretty sure there was a cupcake crushed beneath his hip, but he was too comfortable to move. They could deal with that later.

"Uh, that didn't quite go how I'd planned," she finally said.

"No?" Asher picked up his head, just enough so that he could look down at her, a single eyebrow raised in question. "Exactly how did you think that would go down?"

"Oh, you know, I had this vision of myself as an amazon princess, holding you down, torturing you with icing until I finally had you begging for mercy and promising never to call any woman cupcake again."

A bubble of laugher rolled up from deep inside his chest. There was nothing about Kennedy Duchane that was boring.

"Apparently you forgot to take my battle-honed skills into account."

Her lips quirked into a half smile. "Apparently."

"Although, I'm hardly going to complain about your methods of torture. They were a hell of a lot more pleasant than anything else I've endured."

Asher didn't realize what he'd said until Kennedy went utterly still beside him.

"The fact that you can talk about being tortured so flippantly makes me…"

This time he let her words hang in the air, curious to see just how she'd finish the sentence.

"Crazy and scared and pissed and like I should kiss you all over."

"Pretty sure you just did that."

Kennedy shoved at his shoulder. He let his body rock back with the momentum, using it to press her tighter against his chest.

He didn't need the kind of balm she was offering, his scars were long past healed, but it was nice that someone was finally making the offer.

Looking back, he'd rarely had anyone in his life to give a damn. Sure, his grandma had loved him. And even if her methods for keeping a headstrong and sullen teenager in line had been high-handed at times, he'd always known her discipline had come from a place of affection.

His ex-wife had been many things, but nurturing wasn't one of them. At the time, he hadn't particularly thought he needed that.

Maybe he'd been wrong.

"It bothers me that you fall back on bland comments or humor to deflect topics you don't like."

The fact that she noticed should have bothered him. It was a defense mechanism he hadn't even been aware of until a few years ago. Kennedy understanding him enough to recognize that left him vulnerable.

Which only made him want to make another quip to force her away from anything resembling the heavy topic she was hell-bent on tackling.

But he didn't. Instead, he gave her the truth.

"Yes, I've been tortured. Shot and stabbed. I've had broken bones and minor lacerations. Comes with the territory. But I'm fine now."

Pressing up onto her elbow, Kennedy watched him for several seconds. "I'm not sure your definition of fine and mine are the same. You don't let anyone in."

Seriously, this woman saw too damn much.

"What do you mean? I have Jackson and Knox. You—" he quickly tacked something onto that single word before she realized it meant more than he'd intended "—and the rest of the Trident team."

"Work. Is that all you have in your life? Work and meaningless sexual encounters with women you know you'll never see again?"

Asher spread his hands across her hips and lifted her up and off of him. "I'm not talking about other women while you're naked and draped across me, Kennedy."

A small smile tugged at the edge of her lips.

Climbing out of bed, Asher couldn't explain why he suddenly felt as if a band was clamped around his ribs. He needed to get out of here, away from this conversation.

"I'm gonna wash the rest of this sugar off. Join me?"

"You know I'm not that easily distracted."

He tossed her a wicked grin and pointed at the crumbling mess of cupcake in the bed they'd just shared. "That would suggest otherwise, cupcake."

Kennedy growled a warning he had no intention of heeding.

"Surely you realize I'm not going to just let this go."

Snagging a cupcake off the plate, Asher shoved half of it into his mouth. An eyebrow cocked in challenge, he strode across the cabin for the tiny bathroom attached.

Kennedy trailed behind him. She dropped the lid down over the toilet, wrapping her legs up into a pretzel as she watched him from her perch.

Asher flipped on the water as hot as it would go, trying not to let himself be distracted by Kennedy and her beautiful, naked body.

"You have to be carrying around some psychological weight from the things you've done and seen."

Shaking his head, he ducked into the shower, closing the clear glass door between them. It didn't help.

Why was she digging? Why did she care, when she was just going to walk out of his life?

Tipping his head back beneath the hot stream, Asher closed his eyes…and eventually answered her. "Sure, it bothers me sometimes. I mean, I wouldn't be human if it didn't. I killed people, Kennedy. We all did. But it was either kill or be killed. And while I'd like to think everything I did, every order I followed, fell firmly in the white areas of clearly good, I know that we operated mostly in the gray. The SEALs aren't called in for the piddly shit. We handle life and death, national security."

He didn't want to see her reaction, but he couldn't

stop himself from reaching out and running his palm across the glass, wiping away a clear patch through the steam and fog built up on the surface.

Part of him wished he hadn't.

Kennedy watched him, her whiskey eyes somehow sad and fierce. He didn't want to see that expression on her face, especially after the amazing encounter they'd just shared.

After several seconds, she unfolded her lithe body. He watched her step across the small space and reach for the handle on the shower door.

She slid inside with him, closing the glass behind her and cloaking them both in the rising bubble of steam.

She didn't touch him, which was a damn feat, considering how small the shower was. She stared up at him and in a quiet voice said, "Thank you."

"For what?"

"Everything. The sacrifices you made. Putting your life on the line. Bringing my brother home safe and whole. Giving me the most amazing orgasm in my life and making sure I'll never look at a cupcake the same way again. For being the man you are."

A lump formed in the back of his throat. Shit. She was going to make him care.

That band of pressure squeezed harder. Hope and fear, an uncomfortable combination, seemed to itch beneath his skin. Suddenly, he was restless and needy.

As if sensing he was floundering, Kennedy fell back on the defense mechanism she always used, the one that had apparently deserted him just when he'd needed it most.

Her mouth tipping up in a saucy smile, she said, "But I'm still not okay with you calling me cupcake."

Asher laughed, the sound of it echoing off the walls and bouncing back at both of them.

Wrapping his arms around her body, he tugged her tight against him. Burying his nose in her soft hair, he said, "You realize that's not going to stop me, right?"

Kennedy sighed, a single exasperated word gushing across his wet skin. "Yep."

14

SOMETHING BETWEEN THEM had shifted. Kennedy had felt it, cocooned inside that small, quiet room, alone with Asher. Several days later, sitting beside him on another plane, the echo of it was still reverberating through her body.

Scaring her straight down to her bones.

For the better part of two years they'd sniped and barely tolerated each other. But now... There was something about seeing Asher at his most vulnerable, knowing that *she* was the only one able to help him through a difficult situation, that called to a place deep inside her.

But no matter what, she couldn't let that spot grow. Because there wasn't a future here. Not when she was leaving. Not when Asher had given her no indication that this meant more to him.

So her developing emotions were her own issue to deal with.

After almost two weeks on the *Amphitrite*, they were now returning to their real lives. They still had several more days of filming at the Trident main offices, but when this was over...they would be, too.

She'd be starting a new adventure far from home, something she'd wanted for a very long time. A month ago, if anyone had told her that landing her dream job would suddenly feel like a burden instead of a blessing, she would have laughed in their face. But today, she didn't like the churning sensation in her belly whenever she thought about leaving for Seattle.

The plane touched down on the runway. Asher's leg rubbed against hers as he shifted in his seat. How much different this ride had been from their flight out.

On the way to the Bahamas, tension had twisted her gut. This time, somewhere over the Caribbean Sea she'd fallen asleep with her head resting against Asher's shoulder. At some point he'd shifted her body, tucking her into his side and giving her a solid place to snuggle into his warmth.

A sharp pain pinched her chest as he stood, gathering their bags from the overhead bin and shouldering them both without even asking her. Because that was the kind of guy he was.

She followed behind, shuffling into the aisle ahead of him when he dropped back to hold the line of people trying to push past.

They hadn't checked any luggage, so it was a quick trip through customs and out into the muggy Florida heat.

Stopping at her car in the garage, Asher waited for her to fish her keys from her purse and unlock the trunk. He loaded her things and closed it again, pressing his hip against the side.

Arms crossed over his chest, he studied her for several seconds.

"Come home with me."

They were the first words he'd spoken to her in about an hour. Kennedy tried not to let her heart gallop at them. A lump formed in the back of her throat, but she pushed it down and forced herself to say the words she knew she must.

Distance, she needed some if she had any hope of getting out of this thing with her heart intact.

"I have to go home and unpack. Check on things. Get Max from the vet. He's been cooped up there long enough."

"Bring Max with you."

God, she was weak. Because she wanted to do just that. But how long would this last? A few more days? A week at the most.

Pushing away from the car, Asher snagged her, pulling her against his body. He was strong, solid. Tempting. His scent wrapped around her just as surely as his arms. And she wanted him, not only physically, although her body was definitely responding to him. But everything he was willing to give her for as long as she could get it.

Hands on her hips, Asher pushed her back against the car. His palms settled on either side of her head, trapping her. The thing was, she didn't want to get free.

That moment, that place, was exactly where she wanted to be.

And what was so bad about that? At least for right now.

She could deal with the aftermath of her decision later, when she didn't have any other choice.

Asher brought his mouth to hers, coaxing, slow and devastating. He teased her lips, brushing softly and licking, until she couldn't help but open to him. With a few well-placed moves, he had her panting. In the middle of a public parking garage.

What was it about this man that made her completely lose her head?

"Come home with me, Kennedy. I want you there."

Four little words she was powerless to ignore.

"Damn you," she breathed out even as she nodded her head, giving in.

He chuckled, the sound of it as much of a caress as the little nip of his teeth against her bottom lip. When he pulled back, he was grinning down at her, a wicked heat filling his expressive eyes.

"Get Max. Do whatever you need to. I've got dinner covered. After the stress of the last few days, I think we both deserve an easy, carefree night."

His words were so enticing.

Kennedy watched him walk across the garage to where his Jeep was parked. Throwing his bag into the passenger's seat, he turned and waited until she pulled out before jumping in and following her.

She told herself not to rush. To take her time, check on her condo, throw some laundry into the washer, flip through the mail that had piled up while she was gone.

But none of that happened. Kennedy tossed her bag inside the front door, raced around throwing a few toiletries and a change of clothes into another bag, and was back out the door in about twenty minutes flat.

It took another thirty to retrieve Max, the blue heeler and lab mix she'd adopted from the pound a year ago. He was the most loyal dog she'd ever seen and had made moving from her childhood home to her own place after graduation a little less lonely.

Less than an hour and a half after leaving him at the airport, Kennedy pulled into Asher's driveway.

And just sat there, staring at his front door, her heart thumping a mile a minute.

It was one thing to let him into her life and body when they were cocooned on the *Amphitrite*. But she was about to cross a line. And she knew it was a bad idea but couldn't stop herself from doing it anyway. Beside her, Max whimpered, confused about what they were doing and where they were.

"Right there with you, buddy."

Before she could change her mind, the dark blue front door opened, framing Asher's large body. His wide shoulders practically filled the frame, not that he stayed there long.

A few frantic heartbeats later he was striding down the walk and straight toward her car. He made a hand gesture, which she assumed meant he wanted her to roll down her window. So she did.

Leaning down, he loomed over her.

"Turn off the car, Kennedy."

Dropping her head back against the seat, she twisted so that she could look up at him. From her vantage point he looked dark and dangerous. But there, deep in his eyes, she could see remnants of the lost little boy he'd given her glimpses of over the past several days.

And that was her weakness. Realizing he wasn't as invincible as she'd always assumed.

What was giving in to this going to cost her? Because sitting here, staring up at Asher, she knew she was going to pay at some point. But she couldn't quite convince herself the price wouldn't be worth it.

Kennedy's fingers played with the keys dangling

from her ignition for several seconds before finally flipping the car off. The engine died. Asher grabbed the handle and opened the door. Reaching across her, he took a few seconds to scratch Max behind the ears, right where he liked.

His throat was in front of her face. Thick, tanned and tempting. Her mouth watered, and she was tired of fighting against what she wanted.

Leaning forward, she placed her lips to his warm skin and enjoyed the way he sucked in a harsh breath. But that was the only reaction he gave her.

His hand found hers, interlacing their fingers together. Applying light pressure, Asher urged her out.

He grabbed Max's leash and led them both into his home. She'd always known where he lived, but had never been inside. The guys got together regularly, but she'd never been invited over for those male-bonding moments.

Kennedy had expected the place to be...bare. Not necessarily lacking in furnishings, but she'd always assumed Asher was a minimalist, industrial kind of guy.

Instead, his home seemed...lush. The sectional taking up most of the den was a deep, dark brown leather, but it looked so buttery soft. And there was color, a bright green that reminded her of his eyes, dark red with a few splashes of white and tan to lighten things up. There were knickknacks everywhere.

Dropping his hand, she walked across the room to a shelf with a series of unusual objects on display. A green glass frog, a tribal mask, something metal that looked as if it had been blown apart on one end. Pieces of art that had been handcrafted.

"Where did all of these come from?"

He shrugged, coming up beside her, shoving his hands deep inside the pockets of his khaki shorts. "I like to pick up things wherever I go. Reminders of the places I've been and the people I've met. We were often in small villages or poorer countries. I tried to buy from the local artists whenever I could."

Kennedy stared at him for several seconds, fighting the urge to kiss him, before turning back to study each item. The craftsmanship in each piece was amazing. It was clear they'd been given a place of honor.

Turning to him, Kennedy said, "Your ex-wife is an idiot."

Asher blinked and then did it again. There was a part of her that delighted in knocking him a little off-kilter. Although it hardly made up for the fact that she always felt one step behind when he was close.

"Thanks. I think."

"Trust me, it was a compliment."

He just shook his head and then spun on his heel, heading for the open kitchen across from the den. She followed, pulling up a stool at the island in the center of the large space.

The dark stone countertops gleamed, along with the stainless appliances. If she couldn't see the timer on the oven counting down and two pots sitting on the hot stove, she might have assumed the kitchen was spotless because it never got used.

Asher grabbed a bowl, filled it with water and placed it on the floor for Max to drink. He moved through the room, opening drawers and grabbing utensils, handling them with an assurance that only came from experience.

So the man could cook.

"Is there anything you're not good at?"

He looked up from stirring something in a skillet that was letting off a heavenly scent of cream and garlic.

He laughed. "You're good for my ego."

Kennedy's mouth twisted into a wry smile.

"Well, you're going to ruin me for other guys. No one in Seattle will ever be able to live up to the standard you're setting. I would have been just fine with ordering a pizza or picking up takeout."

Asher stilled, and Kennedy realized just what she'd said. There was a part of her that waited, for him to make a joke, say she shouldn't leave, something, anything...

Several seconds ticked past with nothing. Finally, he looked up at her, that wicked grin tugging at his lips, and said, "I have faith the men in Seattle will step up to the plate."

His words hurt. Much more than she wanted them to, but that was her problem, and she wasn't going to ruin the time she did have with him by letting the pain rule her.

Turning away, Asher picked up a bottle of cabernet and poured them both a glass. He pulled a salad from the fridge and plated some pasta with a mouth-watering cream sauce. When he opened the oven, the scent of perfectly cooked steak hit her full force, making her stomach rumble loudly.

Asher chuckled.

Sitting at the table a few moments later, Kennedy groaned as she put the first bite into her mouth. He flipped her a cocky grin, so she retaliated by tossing her napkin at his head. "Show-off."

"Says the girl who sounds like she's making love to my food."

She shrugged, too caught up in the wonderful meal to argue with him.

They talked and ate, the evening flowing easily around them. It was unexpected but nice. Seductive.

It almost made her feel as if they were actually dating, and that was dangerous. The thought was too enticing.

Leaning back into his chair, Asher called Max over and shared a couple of bites of steak he'd saved.

"You're going to spoil him." She'd meant the words to be light and teasing, but apparently that wasn't how he took them.

Turning, he pinned her with those dangerous green eyes. "Probably, but I honestly don't care. I've learned life is too short to worry about things like that. You have to take the moments when they're in front of you, because you might not get another chance."

For long stretches at a time Kennedy could forget all that this man had seen and experienced. The grief and fear and danger. And then he said something like that, and it all came crashing back.

"I'm so glad you're out of the SEALs."

He folded his arms on the table in front of him and leaned closer. "Why?"

"I just…it bothers me, thinking about what you and Jackson and Knox risked every day. How close you guys all came to danger. The burdens you'll all carry for the rest of your days."

Kennedy glanced down at the table, the emotions she'd fought so hard while her brother had been gone welling up fresh and real, as if he was still off being a soldier and putting his life on the line.

"I hated it. Knowing each day could mean someone

showing up on the front porch to tell us he was gone. And I hated myself for being selfish. I knew what Jackson was doing was important. Brave and honorable."

"But you couldn't stop wishing he could be safe."

"Exactly."

Asher stood, grasped her hand and pulled her up from the table. Kennedy resisted, feeling fragile and unexpectedly brittle. But he wouldn't let her go.

"I get it. I lived the same thing until my dad died. And felt guilty as hell for being angry at him when I was younger. I needed someone to blame. My mom was gone, and my grandma hardly spoke of her. But my dad…his memory was a physical presence in my life. He was there, but not. And it was easy to blame him, to feel he'd made a choice that took him away from me and left me alone."

Kennedy sucked in a harsh breath. Her chest ached, for the boy he'd been and the man he'd grown into.

How could she have worked with Asher for two years and not realized that the cocky exterior hid such a wounded soul?

Going up on her toes, Kennedy pressed her mouth to his. The kiss was soft, soothing. His hands on her shoulders tightened, but before he could deepen the moment, she pulled away.

That wasn't what the kiss had been for.

And she needed to pull back into herself before she went too far and couldn't retreat anymore.

Kennedy squirmed in his hold, trying to get free. "Let me get the dishes. You cooked, so it's the least I can do."

"Leave them," he said, holding tight.

Panic bubbled up, sure and perilous. If she let him

touch her right now, the last barrier she'd managed to keep in place would crumble away. And she didn't think she could handle that. She was already hanging on by a thread.

Tears pricked the backs of her eyes, burning. Closing them, Kennedy tried to hold the emotions back, but Asher was too damn perceptive.

"Hey," he whispered, dragging her into the shelter of his body. "He's safe."

He thought she was upset over Jackson's years in the SEALs, and it would be smart if she let him keep that perception. But it wouldn't be honest, and she didn't want lies, even of omission, between them.

"That's not what's wrong."

"Then, what?"

She shook her head. "I'm just…feeling overwhelmed, I guess. It's been a crazy few months, and the next week is going to go so quickly."

His fingers threaded through her hair, the warmth of his palm cupping the base of her neck. His thumb beneath her chin, Asher applied pressure until she looked up at him.

She'd been avoiding his gaze, but now she couldn't. He looked the way she felt…somber. And she hated herself a little for ruining the moment.

Asher tugged on her hand, pulling her across the room until they were both settled on the couch. The TV came on, some mindless show neither of them particularly cared about.

He stretched his legs out and positioned Kennedy between his open thighs. She dropped her head back against his chest.

She'd dated, had a few boyfriends over the years.

But none of them had ever made her feel this…safe. Accepted. Protected.

A knot twisted in her belly. Why did she have to find this now, when her entire life was about to change?

She'd watched friends—from high school and college—change their dreams and plans because of a man. And she'd always promised herself that was something she'd never do. Any man who wanted her would accept her life the way she lived it.

Maybe, finally, she was beginning to understand.

Because in that moment, if Asher had asked her to stay, she might have agreed.

15

GOD, HOLDING HER like this, snuggled up on the couch watching mindless television, it would be so easy to let Kennedy into his life.

But that wasn't possible.

When Krista had left, he'd promised himself he'd never open himself to that kind of pain again. But it was entirely possible Kennedy had the ability to hurt him a hell of a lot worse than Krista ever had.

He was in over his head. Walking out of the airport, he'd known he needed to let her go. It was the logical time to end things. And that's what he'd planned to do.

But when push had come to shove, he hadn't been able to do it.

His palms had started sweating, and his mind had raced. His heart had pounded, and a sick sludge had churned deep in his belly. Until he'd touched her, and then all those symptoms had disappeared.

Having her here, in his home, felt right.

He wanted Kennedy in his bed. His physical need for her was overwhelming and elemental.

Asher's fingers played over her body, tripping softly

along her skin. There was something powerful about the way she melted against him, trusting him with her body as she relaxed.

Kennedy shivered, his fingers dancing across her skin, slipping inside the neckline of her shirt. She'd worn a pair of tiny white shorts that showed off her tanned legs. And a cotton shirt with a muted floral print and small white buttons up the front.

He paused at the first one, giving her a chance to tell him to stop before he popped it free. Instead, she arched against him, offering up her body for anything he wanted to do.

Making quick work, Asher spread her shirt open, revealing the light pink bra beneath and the silver clasp holding it closed between her breasts.

Her hands settled on the inside of his thighs, and through the fabric of his shorts, her fingernails scraped softly up and down. Twisting, her lips found the underside of his jaw and kissed. Nipped. Sucked.

Asher popped the catch, letting her breasts spill free into his waiting palms. Her nipples were already tight, begging him for attention. Rolling one between his thumb and forefinger, he relished the way her breath caught.

He wanted to go slowly with her, but his hands were already shaking, and he didn't think he had it in him. Not right now. Maybe later, after that first sharp edge of need had been dulled.

Lifting her high, he placed her feet on the floor and quickly pulled the rest of her clothes off, revealing her luscious body. She stood in front of him, hands braced on his shoulders, and watched him.

Spreading his thighs wide, Asher pulled her into the

open V and rained kisses across her skin. She swept her fingers into his hair and tugged, not enough to hurt but enough to get his attention.

Dropping his head back, he stared up at her and waited. There was something in the way she watched him, hope, fear and hesitation all mixed together.

He was about to reach for her clothes when she gripped the back of his shirt in her fist and pulled it off over his head. Lifting his hips, he helped her open the front of his shorts and push them out of the way, grabbing a condom out of his wallet before tossing them away.

Her hands trailed across his body, as if she couldn't stop touching him. As if she'd never get enough. If only that were true. A few short days from now she'd walk away...like every other woman in his life.

Climbing back onto the couch, Kennedy spread her thighs wide, bracketing his hips.

She was soft and fragrant. Warm and welcoming.

The heat of her sex rubbed against his throbbing erection. She was wet, the evidence of her desire leaving him slick.

Sweeping his hands through her hair, Asher pulled it back, wanting to see her face, watch her expression. And there was something there. Something deep inside those whiskey eyes that made his throat tighten and chest ache even as she reached between them, guiding him to the entrance of her body.

Slowly, she sank down, taking him deep. Asher's eyelids closed, blocking out everything except the pure feel of her.

"I don't think I'll ever get used to how perfect you

feel," he growled, his hands on her flexing to bring her closer.

He held them both still for several seconds, simply soaking up their connection. The warmth of her broken, passion-saturated breaths. Her spicy, sweet scent filling him up. He wanted to savor this. Her. Them.

But Kennedy wasn't content with that. Her hips began to move, and Asher was powerless to fight the friction and rhythm she was creating.

He followed her pace, enjoying the freedom to run his hands across her body, to suck her nipples into his mouth. He could feel her tighten, muscles clamping around him deep inside her body.

They were both panting, quickly reaching the edge of patience, wanting more. Asher's hands were on her hips, urging her faster, harder. The soft sounds of her whimpers roared through his head. Her body trembled against him. God, he loved it when she trembled with need, searching for the relief only he could give her.

But tonight, he wanted more than an orgasm, no matter how mind-blowing it might be.

"Look at me," he said.

Kennedy's eyes popped open, glowing tawny brown, and immediately found his. Chest to chest, so close, there was no avoiding the emotions building between them, right along with the impending orgasm.

There was no hiding. Asher might feel the most vulnerable in his entire life, but in that moment, he wasn't the only one open and bare.

What he saw in Kennedy's gaze gave him a burst of hope. She wanted him. Felt something for him, the same deep connection he'd been desperately fighting.

Maybe, maybe...

The thought spiraled away, along with the crash of Kennedy's release. Her body clamped hard around him. His hips bucked against hers, even as she ground down against him, milking every speck of pleasure from the moment.

Her lips opened, sighed a single word...his name.

The way she looked, lost in ecstasy, his name on her lips...it was too much. His own body shuddered and then exploded, everything spilling out with several deep, hard thrusts that left him spent.

At some point her fingers had tangled in his hair. Her heated skin pressed against him, but he never wanted her to move.

If he could, Asher would stay in that moment forever.

But reality slowly encroached. Somewhere behind them, Max perked up from his spot on the floor, the tags on his collar jingling an alert that came about thirty seconds too late.

The side door, the one all of his friends used to walk straight into his place, opened and slammed shut.

And a voice rang out, "Hey, man, what's Kennedy's car doing in your driveway?"

OH SHIT.

Kennedy barely had time to react, her brain still cloudy from what she and Asher had just shared. But she didn't really need to do anything because the minute her brother's voice sounded, Asher was in motion.

She was off his lap, on her feet, and the shirt he'd been wearing not an hour ago pulled over her head and dangling past her thighs.

Asher was zipping up his shorts when Jackson

crossed the threshold into the room and stopped mid-stride.

Her brother's quick gaze swept across the scene, taking in every little detail that told a story difficult to misinterpret.

A crease wrinkled the spot right between his eyebrows. His words were slow and deliberate when he asked, "What the hell is going on?"

Part of her expected Asher to distance himself, to put as much space between them as humanly possible. Instead, he stepped right up to her, his chest to her back, and wrapped a possessive arm tight around her.

The frown tugging at Jackson's lips deepened as he rounded the couch. He didn't stop until he was looming over her, face-to-face with Asher.

"She's my sister," he growled.

Asher applied pressure, urging her to the left, out from between the two of them.

"I'm aware of that," he said, his voice low and even. "But it isn't what you think."

"No? So I'm wrong in assuming one of my best friends, a guy I've bled with and fought with, just got finished screwing my sister?"

Kennedy watched the blood drain from Asher's face. And then it all flooded back, burning red with anger and indignation.

Crap.

The last thing she needed was for Asher to lose his temper and deck Jackson.

And she refused to be the reason these two friends came to blows. Especially now that she understood just how important Jackson and Knox were to Asher, how alone he would be without these brothers.

Pushing between them, Kennedy put her palms in the center of Jackson's chest and shoved. He didn't move much, but it was enough. At least she had his attention.

Jackson's gaze shifted from Asher to her, and for a few seconds she wished it hadn't.

The anger and anguish there sent a bolt of pain through her own chest. She could handle just about anything, except her brother's disappointment.

"This isn't his fault, Jackson."

"No? Then it's yours?"

"It's no one's fault. We're both adults, perfectly capable of deciding who to let into our beds."

Jackson glared at her, his laser-blue gaze cutting straight through her. "Maybe, although you don't exactly have a great track record where lovers are concerned, do you, Kennedy? Indecent exposure, really?"

Kennedy gasped. It was her turn for the blood to drain from her face. She felt light-headed, and the room began to spin. Heavy hands gripped her shoulders, holding her still and anchoring her in place, when, for a few seconds, it felt as if her entire world had exploded.

"How, how did you know?" She twisted around, glaring at Asher. "Did you tell him?"

"No," he growled, his gaze thunderous.

"He didn't," Jackson tossed a glare at his friend and then ran his hands through his hair, tugging at it several times before looking at her again. "Did you really think I wouldn't keep tabs on you? You're my only sister, Kennedy. I have specialized skills and friends all over the place. Of course I knew what was going on with you."

But... "Why didn't you ever say anything?"

"Because I figured if you wanted my help you'd come to me. I wanted you to trust me with the truth, but you never did. You're not great at letting people in." His lips twisted into an unhappy frown. "It's a trait you share with him."

Kennedy turned her head, looking at Asher over her shoulder. Jackson wasn't wrong.

"You're both strong-willed and stubborn as hell. Cautious even though you like to pretend that reluctance is by choice and not because of past experiences."

God, he was right.

"You don't have to worry about this affecting our work. Even though there are still a couple days of filming, it's temporary. I'm leaving for Seattle in less than a week, after all."

Instead of calming him down, that only made Jackson glare at her even more.

"Just one more reason this was a bad idea. But I guess it's too late to stop it, now."

Spinning on his heel, Jackson disappeared through the door he'd entered. It might have made her feel better if he'd slammed it, but he didn't.

Guilt, fear and pain rose inside her, a churning sludge that made her belly cramp.

Behind her, Asher dropped onto the sofa. The springs groaned in protest, but he didn't seem to notice. Instead, he scraped both hands up and down his face, as if he could wipe out the past several minutes.

Walking over, Kennedy crouched in front of him, placing her hands on his knees.

Asher moved his legs away from her touch, letting her hands fall empty on to the sofa. The one where they'd just spent the past hour snuggling. Making love...

He didn't even bother looking at her when he muttered, "Go home, Kennedy."

"I'm going to fix this, Asher. I promise. I'll talk to Jackson, smooth things over. I won't let him get upset with you for something I chose to do."

When he didn't respond, Kennedy reached for his hands, prying them away from his face. When he finally looked at her, his expression was completely blank.

"There's n-n-nothing to fix. You'll be leaving in a few days. And I can handle your brother. But he's right and this is over. So, go home."

A hard lump formed in her throat. Kennedy tried to swallow it back, but it wouldn't budge. Something told her neither would Asher. At least, not tonight.

KENNEDY'S WORDS HURT, more than he wanted them to.

They were the reminder he'd desperately needed, especially after making love to her on the couch. He hadn't meant to, but he'd been powerless to hold anything back.

And for a brief moment, he'd thought maybe she'd felt the same soul-stirring connection he had.

But she hadn't.

To her, what they'd shared was just sex and nothing more. In a few days, she'd be gone, and once again, he'd be left shattered.

A sharp pain lanced through his chest, but Asher ignored it. He was used to pain. Could handle it just fine. And this would be no different.

Kennedy stared at him, the expression in her eyes nearly killing him. Anguish. Regret. He didn't want her regret. He wanted her to stay.

"I'm sorry," she whispered.

He wasn't certain what she was apologizing for, but it really didn't matter.

Words raced through his head. Things he could say to change the outcome. But he didn't want to convince her to stay. He needed her to want to be with him. Was it too much to ask that someone, anyone, would choose him?

"Go home," he said again, his voice even.

She stared up at him, hesitation in her gaze, and for a second he thought maybe, just maybe, he was wrong. That she was going to wrap her arms around him and say she didn't want to leave.

Instead, she gathered her things, put her clothes back on and walked up beside him. Her soft hand rested on his arm. The heat from her body radiated out, touching him as surely as any caress she could have given him. And his traitorous dick responded, wanting nothing more than to be buried deep inside her again.

He longed for that physical connection, even though he knew now that it was empty.

"I won't let this ruin your friendship or jeopardize your business, Asher. That I promise you."

He didn't give a damn about the business.

"It's fine," he said, even if deep down he knew it wasn't.

She squeezed his arm, holding on just a few seconds longer.

And then she was gone.

16

ASHER WALKED THROUGH the front door of Trident the next morning. After a long, sleepless night, his resolve was set in stone.

Kennedy was leaving. And he wasn't sure he would have stopped her even if he could. This was a major opportunity for her. She'd put all of her time and energy into Trident, but the diving company wasn't her dream. It was Jackson's and Knox's really. And his family.

She deserved the chance to make her own mark on the world. And if he really cared about her, he couldn't stop her from doing that. Even if it hurt.

But for his own peace of mind, he had to stop their relationship. It was going to be difficult enough to let her go. The more time he spent with her, the deeper in he got.

Unfortunately, it wasn't going to be easy to avoid her.

They still had several more days of filming before the documentary crew was finished with them both.

Starting this morning.

Kennedy's car was already in the parking lot, so he knew she was there. And so was Jackson's. At least he'd be able to get all of the difficult conversations over with at once.

He ignored the production crew as he stalked past the front conference room where they'd assembled. Daniel called out to him, but Asher didn't acknowledge the other man.

He was on a mission.

He stopped in the doorway to Kennedy's office, not bothering to knock before entering and closing the door behind him.

Plopping into the chair across from her, Asher put his feet up on her desk, knowing it would drive her absolutely insane.

She glanced at the soles of his boots and then followed the line of his legs straight up his body. Asher felt the impact of her study as if she'd caressed him, but he ignored the physical fallout.

"Look, given the situation, I think it's best if we end whatever this is between us."

Kennedy's mouth opened and closed. Her lips thinned, and her eyes narrowed. But she didn't argue with him. The tiny seed of hope he'd been powerless to stomp out last night finally withered and died.

"We both knew it was nothing more than some fun. But you're leaving, and my relationship with Jackson is more important than some fling, even if the sex was stellar."

He watched Kennedy's face blanch and then blaze bright red. But she slowly nodded.

"We have a few more days of filming. Help me get through them, and then we can both move on with our lives."

He didn't wait for Kennedy to respond but bounded

up from the chair and turned to leave. However, two steps into the hall, he was startled to be grabbed by the arm and spun into an empty office, his back slammed against the wall.

"I should put my fist through your face for that," Jackson growled at him, the fist in question poised for action and aimed straight at his nose.

"You want to punch me because I broke things off with her, but you didn't when you walked into my house and found her practically naked in my living room?"

Jackson's fist wavered before dropping. Using both hands, he shoved Asher's shoulders, driving him harder into the wall.

"Last night you had your arm wrapped around her waist, ready to go toe-to-toe with me in order to protect her. In there, you were just being cruel."

Asher opened his mouth to argue but shut it again. Because maybe Jackson was right. He could have been gentler about ending things, but she'd hurt him, and part of him wanted to hurt her as well.

Shaking his head, he let his body sag against the wall. He was tired.

"Damn," Jackson breathed out. "You actually love her, don't you?"

Asher shook his head, trying to force the words away. He couldn't. He didn't.

Lying to Jackson was useless, anyway. "Yes," he mumbled. "But she's leaving in a few days, so it doesn't really matter."

Wrapping a hand around Asher's neck, Jackson pulled him into a light embrace. "You realize you're an idiot, right?"

"For falling for your sister? Yeah, I'm aware."

Jackson just shook his head.

THE THREE DAYS that followed were pure torture. If she'd thought Asher could be an asshole before, that was nothing compared to the way he'd been acting since they'd returned to work.

She was ready to kill him, and she thought Daniel was close to putting out a professional hit.

Where was the guy she'd gotten to know on the ship? Had he been a figment of her imagination? Had he been putting on an act just to get inside her pants? Kennedy didn't want to believe it.

Mercifully, there was finally a light at the end of the tunnel. This evening was the last day of filming. After this, the project would wrap, and she'd be free to concentrate on the details of her move to Seattle. She already had a Realtor searching for apartments, so she could hit the ground running when she arrived.

Daniel had shot Asher a pointed glare when he'd finally arrived, showing up two hours after their original call time. He'd walked into Trident in the same clothes he'd left in the day before, his hair a mess, bags under his eyes and reeking of perfume.

Kennedy had felt sick. Unable to stick around and watch, she'd fled to Jackson's office and hid out there for a little while.

She and Jackson had gone over the few items she needed to pass on before leaving Trident, which meant that, as soon as filming was complete, her employment with Trident would be finished.

And several hours later, she couldn't continue to hide, not when her place was out there with the production crew. It was late, already dark outside, so they had to be close to finished.

Her body braced for whatever was coming her way, Kennedy walked into the conference room the crew had been using and stopped short.

"...the pig tore through the camp, trampling tents, ripping through supplies, not even bothering to stop and nose at the food churned up."

Asher sat, his hips propped against the end of the large table sitting in the middle of the room. Jackson was kicked back in one of the chairs, the biggest grin she'd ever seen on his face. They were engrossed in each other and the story she'd walked in on. But their profiles were to the room with the cameras capturing every moment.

Leaning back, Asher laughed, the loud, robust sound echoing through the room. It wasn't until that moment that Kennedy realized she hadn't heard it in days.

"Or the expression on that teenager's face when he walked into that clearing in the middle of the godforsaken jungle only to find twelve semiautomatics trained on his forehead."

This was the man she'd missed for the past several days. The one she'd seen on the *Amphitrite*. The guy she'd thought had been a figment of her imagination.

Tears pricked the backs of her eyes. She must have made some noise, because both Asher's and Jackson's gazes jerked in her direction.

Jackson's grin softened when he looked at her. But Asher...his expression simply shut down.

"Kennedy. I thought you'd already left."

"No. Why would I leave? This is my project, and today's the last day."

Asher's pale green gaze slipped away from her, and she felt the loss of it straight down to the soles of her feet.

"Jackson said you'd turned over all your other projects this afternoon."

Everyone in the room began to shift and murmur. Daniel stepped into the shot, leaning across the table toward both men. "Thanks, guys, I really appreciate you sharing some of your stories with us, even if you couldn't get too specific." Turning back to the crew, he said, "That's a wrap. Asher's invited everyone back to his place for a few beers. You all should have the address."

She hadn't gotten the invite. Kennedy tried not to let that bother her, but it did.

Asher stood up and wandered out without even looking at her.

She was so overwhelmed she didn't even hear Jackson approach until he was standing right beside her, watching the same empty doorway. "He's an idiot."

"Tell me something I don't already know." She flashed her brother a smile but didn't even pretend it was real.

"He's hurting, Kennedy."

"He has a really strange way of showing it."

Jackson shrugged. "I'm not about to fault him for whatever gets him through this, especially since you're the one leaving."

Her brother didn't even wait for her reaction, although she wasn't entirely certain what it would have been. It was clear Jackson was implying that Asher felt more for her than he'd let on. But she didn't believe him. Or maybe didn't want to believe him.

Asher was the one who'd broken things off.

"So, you're heading out to Seattle day after tomorrow?"

Kennedy nodded. She planned on staying out there for a couple weeks, long enough to find a place, meet her new boss and coworkers and then come home to get all of her stuff.

And she was already dreading that goodbye with her father, mother and brother at the airport.

But she needed to do this. For herself. Or she'd always question whether or not she had the strength to stand on her own.

The next two days flew past, a blur of activity as she tried to square away her life in Jacksonville and arrange things in Seattle.

Her stomach was in knots as she boarded the plane, replaying her mom's tears, Dad's gruff goodbye and Jackson's whispered "make sure you come home in one piece" in her ear, the same words she'd spoken to him countless times before.

There was one person she wished had been there, and for a brief moment she thought she'd caught a glimpse of him in the crowd around security, but it had only been her imagination playing awful tricks.

Several hours later, she'd touched down and hit the ground running. Apartments, movers, new company and corporate culture. Everything had been intimidating and overwhelming.

And, if she was honest, disappointing.

Two or three days into her new job, it had become clear that it was not exactly what she'd thought—or been told. Instead of being a junior member of the team, learning the ropes and assisting on major national ad campaigns, she was little more than a glorified fetch-it girl. She handled the grunt work, editing someone else's copy, refining someone else's graphic artwork, researching someone else's campaign ideas, instead of brainstorming her own.

For three weeks Kennedy tried to tell herself this was how things worked. She had to pay her dues and work her way up the chain. But during lunch with one of her new coworkers, she'd come to realize that working her way up the chain at Masters, Dillon and Cooper could take her ten years of sixty- and eighty-hour work weeks, none of which would be spent on her own campaigns.

And maybe, if she hadn't had a taste of something more, she'd have been satisfied with that path. But at Trident she'd had autonomy. She'd headed up her own major marketing campaign, interacted with the media, written press releases, formulated sound bites and spun crises.

It didn't take long for doubts to creep in. Had she made a seriously bad decision?

Adding to that, whenever she thought of home, she remembered Asher and that last night of filming. And she wanted him. Not just physically, although the burning need for his touch was always there. But she wanted his laugh, his confidence, even his stutter, although she'd noticed it had been completely absent during those last few days. At some point in the process, he'd gained confidence in front of the camera and conquered his fear, probably without even realizing.

Kennedy had never been the kind of woman to hold

back, except when it came to love. Jackson wasn't wrong when he said she rarely let anyone in. Because the few occasions she had, things hadn't exactly gone well.

She was scared of trusting the wrong person again. And Asher scared her more than anyone else ever had. He could seriously hurt her.

But was that really a valid reason to not even try?

She knew the answer was no, but taking that leap of faith was harder than she'd ever expected.

Picking up the phone, Kennedy made her weekly call back home, starting with Jackson.

Her brother answered, not even bothering with a hello. "How's Seattle going?"

She wanted to lie to him as she'd been doing since she got here, but tonight the words wouldn't come.

"I…really miss home."

There was a long silence, followed by a chuckle. "Thank God."

"The job is…interesting, but it isn't what I expected. I took it thinking I'd have a chance to use the skills I'd learned, but I'm not, Jackson. I crave the kind of responsibility I had at Trident.

"Real estate is outrageous, and the apartments I can afford don't allow dogs. I miss Max and I'm sure mom and dad will get tired of keeping him at some point. I miss my condo with a view of the water. I miss everyone at Trident. I miss the laid-back atmosphere and sense of family."

"Then, come home."

Jackson made it sound so simple. And maybe it was.

Her heart was back in Jacksonville. The woman who'd left everything behind to travel across the country for a new adventure wouldn't hesitate to go after the man she wanted in her life.

And she wanted Asher.

17

ASHER STARED OUT the windows in his home, watching nothing. Behind him there was a glass of whiskey sitting on the table, ice melting, untouched. The moment he'd poured it he knew it was a mistake...it reminded him of her.

He'd spent the past three weeks trying to prove to himself that he could survive without Kennedy. He wasn't sure anyone was buying the act.

Just this afternoon he'd told Jackson that he planned to take a diving job in Australia. Trident didn't necessarily need the work, but he needed the break. Everywhere he looked, the ghost of Kennedy haunted him.

Maybe a change of scenery would help. God knew he'd attempted to exorcise her with other women, but that hadn't gone well at all. He'd been to bar after bar, but despite being approached by countless women, none of them could hold his attention. And he'd always gone home alone.

Because none of them were Kennedy.

A knock on the door startled him out of the unpleasant thoughts. Frowning, Asher turned away from the view he hadn't really been watching anyway and crossed to the front door, opening it.

Kennedy stared at him, her hands fidgeting at her waist, as if she didn't have a clue what to do with them.

"Wh-what are you doing here, Kennedy?"

Asher ground his teeth together. After everything that had happened between them, the sight of her set him so off balance that he lost his words.

"Can I come in?"

Asher thought about telling her no, but what point would that serve?

Sweeping back an arm, he silently indicated she could enter, and then shut the door behind her.

She stood in the middle of his living room. A sense of déjà vu overwhelmed him, which didn't help to settle the anxiety jangling his nerves. That first night hadn't ended very well. He really didn't have a desire to re-live it.

"You back in Jacksonville to get the last of your things?" he finally asked.

She shook her head and took a single step forward. "I'm here for you."

"For me?"

Kennedy nodded, a brief, jerky movement. What the hell did that even mean?

Turning away, Asher let all of the pain and exhaustion that had been eating him up just pour out of his words. "What do you want, Kennedy?"

He didn't hear her approach, but his entire body bucked when her hands came to rest on his back. He stalled, unable to keep walking away from her, even if his head was screaming at him that it would be better to run.

"I love you." The words came out choked, her voice soft and barely recognizable. His heart thudded unevenly in his chest. Slowly, he turned.

Could this be real? Or had he fallen asleep on the couch again and started dreaming?

"What?"

"I love you. I think I've probably had feelings for you for a long time, since you rescued me that night from jail. But you kept pushing me away."

"Because I couldn't let myself want you."

"I get that. I'm Jackson's little sister and your employee. But on the *Amphitrite* we were able to move past that."

Her hands slipped up his arms, over his chest to rest on either side of his face. "You're a good man, Asher. No matter what happens between us, I want you to know that. Don't let anyone ever convince you that you're not worth everything, because you are."

God, he wanted this. Wanted what she was offering him. But could he trust it?

"How is this going to work, Kennedy? I live here. You live in Seattle. I'm willing to give long distance a shot, but are you? It will be difficult."

She smiled up at him, her gorgeous golden eyes twinkling.

"Do you love me?"

He wanted to say no, knew that it was probably the best way to protect his heart. But he couldn't. "Yes."

Her smile widened, brightening up the gloominess that had entered his life the minute she'd left.

"I resigned my job in Seattle."

"Kennedy," he groaned. "You can't do that. You'll regret your decision at some point, and I don't want you to resent me. I'll…sell my part of Trident. Surely someone in Seattle needs an ex-navy SEAL."

Kennedy laughed, throwing her head back and giving everything she had to the moment. Asher didn't really see what was so damn funny.

Her arms wound around his neck, and, going up on tiptoe, she rained kisses across his face, punctuating each of them with words. "I didn't give up my job for you. Or just for you. Working at Masters, Cooper and Dillon wasn't what I thought. It didn't challenge me or give me a chance to grow the way my position with Trident did. I missed everyone here. Sure, you were a factor in my decision, but not all of it. Trust me, I'll never regret choosing to come home. Especially since you're here."

Asher stared down at Kennedy, hope bleeding through him. Could this really be happening? She'd come home for him.

She'd chosen him. She'd chosen them.

Wrapping his arms around her, Asher boosted her up his body until her legs twined around his hips. She let out another giggle, sinking into his kiss when he sealed his mouth to hers.

They reveled in the moment, adrenaline, excitement and pure joy suffusing him.

Until she pulled back, arms straight, and frowned. "There is one problem, though."

The somber expression on her face had his heart flipping over with dread. "What?"

"My condo's no longer available. I have no place to live, so I'm moving back in with Mom and Dad. How good are you at climbing trees?"

Was she serious? If that was the only problem they encountered…

"Ex-navy SEAL, remember? I'm pretty damn good at climbing whatever you put in front of me. But, that won't be an issue."

"Oh, yeah? Why?"

"Because give me a month, and I'll have convinced you to move in with me."

Kennedy laughed, the tinkling sound the best thing he'd ever heard. "Keep dreaming, frogman. I think we need to take things slowly."

Asher just smirked at her, certain eventually he'd get his way. He knew exactly how to play her body to get a yes from her when he really wanted one.

He wanted Kennedy in his life, in his home, in his bed, because she chose to be there. But he wasn't above providing some enthusiastic incentive.

Sweeping her into his arms, Asher strode down the hallway to introduce her to the bedroom that would eventually be theirs.

Epilogue

IT HAD BEEN a long process, but the dive team had finally begun excavating the hold of the *Chimera* a few weeks ago. It had taken nearly two years from Jackson and Loralei's discovery, but they'd reached the end point. Kennedy stood on the deck of the *Amphitrite*, excitement and anticipation churning in her belly.

Despite how busy everyone was, they'd all made time in their schedules to be present.

Jackson and Loralei had returned from their honeymoon a month ago. Knox and Avery had left their newest project off the coast of Turkey to return to the Caribbean. Avery had finally finished her PhD six months ago, and the two had recently been trying to find a date to get married somewhere in the middle of their crazy work schedules.

Asher had gotten his way, and she'd moved in with him, although it had taken about five months instead of one. And she hadn't regretted the decision a single day. He'd been making noises about rings lately, but so far she was resisting. Not because she didn't want to marry him, but because she liked driving him a little crazy.

She'd probably cave on that point the minute he got down on one knee.

But right now, everyone's focus was on what lay inside the hold of the *Chimera*. This moment was a long time in the making.

Asher walked across the deck, slipping his arm around her waist, and together they strode for the far railing. He tucked her in front of him, positioning his body behind her and wrapping an arm tight around her middle.

Happiness bubbled up inside Kennedy as she leaned against him. Coming back to Jacksonville, Trident and Asher had been the best decision she'd ever made.

The documentary had not only been a success, but had gained them some serious media attention when it aired during prime time on one of the major networks. In fact, they'd had several offers from production companies requesting to be present for this moment.

But Jackson, Knox and Asher had all decided it was more important to share the moment with just the Trident family.

All the attention had meant her job had gotten very busy. So busy they were already discussing the possibility of hiring her a marketing assistant.

"I didn't miss anything, did I?"

Beside them, Loralei said, "Not yet. They've attached the lines to the chest and are about to crank up the crane to lift it."

Months ago the team had discovered a chest inside the hold. The moment pictures of it had appeared on their video screens, excitement had rippled through the team. Today, they were finally ready to raise the chest.

Across the deck, Knox directed the crew operating the crane. Jackson was down with the dive team.

An avalanche of water gushed across the deck as the worn wooden surface broke through. The crane groaned under the weight, swinging it and placing it gingerly onto the deck.

Kennedy's breath backed up into her lungs. After over one hundred and fifty years beneath the water, the thing was delicate, hinges rusted and wood rotten. The smallest impact could make it collapse. As it was, they were going to need to get it into a chemical and water solution pronto to prevent as much erosion as possible from sudden exposure to the air.

But they'd all agreed to open the chest together.

Jackson hauled himself onto the deck, shedding equipment and pushing his wet suit down around his hips as he went. He snagged Loralei's hand, and they joined Kennedy, Asher, Knox and Avery, crowding around the chest.

The wood was dark, having soaked up water and salt. Metal curved along all of the edges, and a large lock held the lid closed.

They'd called in an expert on Civil War era locks. Crouched on the deck, the locksmith made quick work of opening the corroded metal and then stepped back.

Kennedy watched as her brother's gaze traveled from Knox to Asher and finally landed on his new wife.

Leaning down, he pressed his lips to Loralei's. "No matter what's inside, I want you to know you're the treasure I found when we discovered the *Chimera*."

Her sister-in-law sighed, a sweet, soft sound that made Kennedy smile.

Asher's arm wrapped around her, and his lips found the warm curve of her neck.

Across from them, Knox bounced on the balls of his feet. "Let's get this over with. The anticipation is killing me."

"Patience, frogman," Avery said, running her hand down his arm and laughing at him.

Together, all three men stepped forward and grasped an edge of the lid.

The hinges groaned, refusing to budge for several seconds before finally letting go. The lid swung back, and everyone gathered around gasped.

Bright Caribbean sunlight glinted off a small stack of gold bars. Kennedy pressed closer, trying to get a better view.

"Holy shit," she breathed, bracing her hand on Asher's back. She could feel the barely suppressed tremor running just beneath his skin.

"How many bars are there?"

"Twenty or so."

"Anyone know how much money that is?"

Jackson looked up at her, shock widening his gaze as he breathed, "Around ten million dollars."

Nearby, the entire crew began whooping and hollering.

Asher grabbed her by the waist and swung her around. He buried his face in her hair and whispered, "We're set, baby."

Kennedy grinned, pushing away from him so she could look up into his face. "Just remember, cupcake, I loved you long before you were rich. I don't give a damn about the money."

He tangled his fingers in her hair, his expression serious. "I love you more than you'll probably ever know, Kennedy Duchane."

He kissed her, the familiar heat and awareness rolling through her. She'd never get enough of this man. He completed her in every way possible.

Kennedy gripped his wrists, holding on to him. Her heart felt as if it was ready to burst.

The *Chimera* might be the site of tragedy, but over the past two years she'd brought them all together. And that was better than a chest full of gold, better than any treasure Kennedy could imagine.

* * * * *

COMING NEXT MONTH FROM

HARLEQUIN *Blaze*

Available November 17, 2015

#871 A COWBOY UNDER THE MISTLETOE
Thunder Mountain Brotherhood
by Vicki Lewis Thompson
Whitney Jones and Ty Slater are about to give in to red-hot temptation. When she can't get home for the holidays, at least she can make it to the sexy cowboy's bed...and into his heart.

#872 A TASTE OF PARADISE
Unrated!
by Leslie Kelly and Shana Gray
2 stories in 1! Warm beaches, cool waves and hot, hot nights—turn up the heat with two scorchingly sexy vacation romances!

#873 TRIPLE DARE
The Art of Seduction
by Regina Kyle
Firefighter Cade Hardesty has never been a one-woman man. His whirlwind affair with photographer Ivy Nelson is hotter than a four-alarm blaze—but can he convince her there's more to it than just sparks?

#874 COWBOY PROUD
Wild Western Heat
by Kelli Ireland
Cade Covington hires PR whiz Emmaline Graystone to promote his new dude ranch. But she can't help her lust for the proud rancher—and keeping things professional is one campaign she might lose.

REQUEST YOUR FREE BOOKS!
2 FREE NOVELS PLUS 2 FREE GIFTS!

HARLEQUIN®

Blaze

red-hot reads!

YES! Please send me 2 FREE Harlequin® Blaze® novels and my 2 FREE gifts (gifts are worth about $10). After receiving them, if I don't wish to receive any more books, I can return the shipping statement marked "cancel." If I don't cancel, I will receive 4 brand-new novels every month and be billed just $4.74 per book in the U.S. or $5.21 per book in Canada. That's a savings of at least 14% off the cover price. It's quite a bargain. Shipping and handling is just 50¢ per book in the U.S. and 75¢ per book in Canada.* I understand that accepting the 2 free books and gifts places me under no obligation to buy anything. I can always return a shipment and cancel at any time. Even if I never buy another book, the two free books and gifts are mine to keep forever.

150/350 HDN GH2D

Name	(PLEASE PRINT)	
Address		Apt. #
City	State/Prov.	Zip/Postal Code

Signature (if under 18, a parent or guardian must sign)

Mail to the **Reader Service**:
IN U.S.A.: P.O. Box 1867, Buffalo, NY 14240-1867
IN CANADA: P.O. Box 609, Fort Erie, Ontario L2A 5X3

Want to try two free books from another line?
Call 1-800-873-8635 or visit www.ReaderService.com.

* Terms and prices subject to change without notice. Prices do not include applicable taxes. Sales tax applicable in N.Y. Canadian residents will be charged applicable taxes. Offer not valid in Quebec. This offer is limited to one order per household. Not valid for current subscribers to Harlequin Blaze books. All orders subject to credit approval. Credit or debit balances in a customer's account(s) may be offset by any other outstanding balance owed by or to the customer. Please allow 4 to 6 weeks for delivery. Offer available while quantities last.

Your Privacy—The Reader Service is committed to protecting your privacy. Our Privacy Policy is available online at www.ReaderService.com or upon request from the Reader Service.

We make a portion of our mailing list available to reputable third parties that offer products we believe may interest you. If you prefer that we not exchange your name with third parties, or if you wish to clarify or modify your communication preferences, please visit us at www.ReaderService.com/consumerchoice or write to us at Reader Service Preference Service, P.O. Box 9062, Buffalo, NY 14240-9062. Include your complete name and address.

HB15

*Ty Slater is a cowboy with a tragic past. And while he's
at Thunder Mountain Ranch to celebrate the holidays
with his foster family, he meets a woman who might just
get past his long-held defenses...*

*Read on for a sneak preview of
A COWBOY UNDER THE MISTLETOE,
the first Christmas story in*
Vicki Lewis Thompson*'s sexy new cowboy saga*
THUNDER MOUNTAIN BROTHERHOOD*.*

They traded the bunched cord back and forth, winding
the lights around the branches until Ty looped the end at
the top. Then they both stepped back and squinted at the
lit Christmas tree to check placement.

"It's almost perfect," Whitney said. "But there's a
blank space in the middle."

"I see it." He stepped forward and adjusted one strand
lower. Then he backed up. "I think that does it."

"I think so, too."

He heard something in her voice, something soft and
yielding that made his heart beat faster. He glanced over
at her. She was staring right back at him, her eyes dark
and her breathing shallow. If any woman had ever looked
more ready to be kissed, he'd eat his hat.

And damned if he could resist her. His gaze locked with
hers and his body tightened as he stepped closer. Slowly
he combed his fingers through hair that felt as silky as he'd
imagined. "We haven't finished with the tree."

"I know." Her voice was husky. "And there's the danc-ing afterward…"

"We were never going to do that." He pressed his fingertips into her scalp and tilted her head back. "But I think we were always going to do this." And he lowered his head.

She awaited him with lips parted. After the first gentle pressure against her velvet mouth, he sank deeper with a groan of pleasure. So sweet, so damned perfect. She tasted like wine, better than wine, better than anything he could name.

The slide of her arms around his waist sent heat shoot-ing through his veins. As she nestled against him, he took full command of the kiss, swallowing her moan as he thrust his tongue into her mouth.

She welcomed him, slackening her jaw and inviting him to explore. He caught fire, shifting his angle and making love to her mouth until they were both breathing hard and molded together. As he'd known, they fit exactly.

The red haze of lust threatened to wipe out his good intentions, but he caught himself before he slid his hands under her sweater. Gulping for air, he released her and stepped back. Looking into eyes filled with the same need pounding through him nearly had him reaching for her again. "Let's… Maybe we should…back off for a bit."

THE WORLD IS BETTER WITH

Romance

Harlequin has everything from contemporary, passionate and heartwarming to suspenseful and inspirational stories.

Whatever your mood, we have a romance just for you!

Connect with us to find your next great read, special offers and more.

f /HarlequinBooks

🐦 @HarlequinBooks

www.HarlequinBlog.com

www.Harlequin.com/Newsletters

H HARLEQUIN®

A *Romance* FOR EVERY MOOD™

www.Harlequin.com

SERIESHALOAD2015